Chill Out with a good book!

To Mr. Auld

From Jessica T.

■SCHOLASTIC

MVP*
*Magellan Voyage Project

MVP✳
✳Magellan Voyage Project

Douglas Evans

pictures by
John Shelley

Front Street
Asheville, North Carolina

For Diane and Tom

Second edition

Library of Congress Cataloging-in-Publication Data

Evans, Douglas
MVP*: *Magellan Voyage Project / Douglas Evans;
pictures by John Shelley.— 1st ed.
p. cm.
Summary: Twelve-year-old Adam Story is challenged by the deposed
ruler of Babababad and his mongoose companion to become the first
youngster to travel around the world in forty days without an adult.
ISBN 1-932425-13-6 (hardcover : alk. paper)
[1. Voyages around the world—Fiction. 2. Voyages and travel—Fiction.
3. Travel—Fiction. 4. Contests—Fiction.
5. Adventure and adventurers—Fiction.]
I. Shelley, John—ill. II. Title.
PZ7.E8775Mag 2004
[Fic]—dc22   2004000506

MVP✻
✻Magellan Voyage Project

Part I
North America

"Home is where the battle lies."

Madam, I'm Adam. I'm twelve years, three months, and twenty-four days old. But this story starts on my birthday, May 1, when I turned twelve. On that day my life changed.

I was sitting outside the After-School Club, surfing the Internet on a school laptop, when I heard footsteps behind me. Turning, I found a short, pudgy man with a flabby neck standing there. He had black hair and wore a black turban with a huge black jewel set in the middle. The rest of his outfit was black as well—black pants, a black silk shirt, and a black cape draped over his shoulders.

"Who wears a cape nowadays?" I asked myself. "Other than magicians, superheroes, and Dracula, I mean."

The After-School Club building was one of those trailer classrooms at the edge of the playground. I stayed there every day until my mother, who worked at the middle school, could pick me up. On my birthday, Mom was running late. I was the only student left, the only witness to this odd visitor.

The man was all nods and grins as he sat at the picnic table. He stared at me with inky black eyes that never blinked. His large neck gave him two chins, the top one rimmed with a thin black beard.

"Happy birthday, Adam Story," he began. His English accent reminded me of actors on educational TV. "It's certainly good to meet you at last. Today, the day you turn twelve, we have certain important issues, certain urgent topics, to discuss. This is an historic day, Adam Story. That's for certain."

Usually I avoided talking to strangers, and this man sure seemed strange. Without a word I began poking the keys on the laptop.

The man reached inside his cape. His hand came out cradling a long, slender animal with a pointed face. Its fur matched the color of a dry playground. The creature's pinpoint eyes ogled me like its master's. Its wide mouth held a slip of paper, a school visitor pass.

"Is that a weasel?" I asked.

The man stroked the creature. "Certainly not. Meet Marco Polo, my mongoose. He's showing you that we're official visitors at your school. Your principal was certain you'd be out here."

The mongoose turned, scurried up the man's arm, and sat on his right shoulder. Its dot eyes never left me.

"Who are you? What do you want?" I asked, fearing that the man was another school counselor eager to know why I never spoke in class, why I never joined in playground games, or why I spent so much time alone at the classroom computer.

Except that this man didn't look like a school district employee.

The visitor snapped his fingers. The mongoose sprang off his shoulder and dove into the cape pocket, then reappeared with a business card in its mouth. The card showed a logo of a wooden sailing ship with the letters "MVP" printed across it and some words underneath:

PRINCE OLIOLI OH XL
PRODUCER, MAGELLAN VOYAGE PROJECT

The look on my face betrayed my doubt.

"Yes, Adam Story," the man said. "As certain as homework, I'm a real prince."

"Why does it say you're XL, extra large?"

"I'm Prince Oh the fortieth. I come from a long line of royalty, an ancient dynasty that ruled over the kingdom of Babababad."

"Babababad? There's no such place," I said, convinced from my web surfing that I knew all one hundred ninety-six countries and kingdoms in the world.

"To be certain, my domain no longer exists," the prince said. "Many centuries ago, a cruel conqueror, Gunter the Hunter, captured Babababad and made it part of his empire. Two centuries later, a European power invaded the empire and turned Babababad into a colony. Three centuries after that, an evil dictator took over the colony, and a century hence, civil wars split it into twenty small republics. Throughout the twentieth century Babababad continued to shrink from takeovers and land deals, until one day a crew simply paved it over for a parking lot. Indeed, Adam Story, although my kingdom cannot be found on certain maps, you can be certain that my royal title has been passed down to me through forty generations."

I reread the business card. In October my fifth-grade class had learned about Ferdinand Magellan, the explorer who led the first fleet of ships that circled the world. But what did Ferdinand have to do with a prince showing up at my school?

"What's the Magellan Voyage Project?" I asked.

The man folded his hands on the tabletop. He wore three silver rings bearing gems as big as the one on his turban.

"For the past year I've traveled the world on behalf of a certain organization called LORD, the League of Royalty without Domains," he began. "I've searched the earth for a certain twelve-year-old boy or girl to join my project, the MVP. I've investigated thousands of youths on every continent. The ideal candidate is someone who has excellent knowledge of the world, someone who is brave but not foolhardy, cunning but not cruel, and cuts a unique path without wandering too far. Most important, Adam Story, I've searched for a twelve-year-old who can stand being alone without being lonely. I'm certain that I've finally found a youth who fits that description. You, Adam Story. You are the certain twelve-year old."

I screwed up my face again. "Certain about what?" I asked. "How do you know anything about me?"

Prince Oh turned his head. He appeared to share a knowing nod with the mongoose on his shoulder.

"For many months, MVP has monitored your computer activity, Adam Story," he said. "We know about the geography and travel web sites you visited. We accessed your library use, and know that every book you checked out was an adventure story. We viewed the list of DVDs you rented and magazines you bought. From the school computer we learned that your mother is employed as a cook in the middle school cafeteria. That's why you can attend schools in this upper-class suburb, even though you live in another town, one where the schools aren't so good. We also know that your grades at this school are outstanding, but you've had a tough time making friends."

"What of it?" I said. "You have no right to hack into my life."

Marco Polo left the prince's shoulder, scurried around his turban, and perched on the other side.

"I'm here to offer you a challenge, Adam Story—an MVP birthday challenge, if you will," Prince Oh said, his black eyes sparkling. "We know you long for travel and yearn for adventure. Well, Adam, my challenge is one of the greatest travel adventures ever offered to a twelve-year-old boy. That's for certain."

A challenge? I had no idea what this prince wanted me to do. Read a bunch of books? Run a race? Participate in one of the dumb "a-thon" fundraisers my school had about once a month?

Prince Oh reached into his cape pocket and took out a PDA, a portable digital assistant, one of those hand-held gadgets. He pressed some tiny buttons and said,

"Check your computer, Adam."

I looked down. A page from the *Encyclopædia Britannica* appeared on the laptop screen. The entry began:

Story, Adam (born May 1, 1992, Concord, CA).

"How'd you do that?" I asked.

"Read on," the prince said.

Story, Adam (born May 1, 1992, Concord, CA). Famous world traveler and adventurer. At age twelve Adam became the youngest person to circumnavigate the globe by land and sea only and without adult accompaniment.

I let out a snort of laughter. "What gives?"

"The challenge, Adam Story," Prince Oh said, pressing more buttons. "History is full of certain individuals who met a certain challenge and became famous for a certain trip. Sally Ride is remembered for her first journey in space. Charles Lindbergh became famous for one flight across the Atlantic Ocean, and every fifth grader learns how Lewis and Clark hiked to the Pacific Ocean one time."

Now the laptop showed the front page of the *San Francisco Chronicle*. The date was August 24 of this year, more than three months into the future. A newspaper headline read:

BOY, 12, YOUNGEST TO CIRCLE WORLD ALONE
Completes Circumnavigation in 40 Days

I shook my head, convinced that this man was a loony.

"Here is the MVP birthday challenge, Adam," Prince Oh said. He sounded very official. "The Magellan Voyage Project challenges you, Adam Story, to travel around the world, without an adult escort, using surface transportation only."

"Right," I said.

"In addition, we challenge you to do it in forty days or less."

I shook my head again. "Come on. Isn't that impossible?"

The mongoose turned a circle on the prince's shoulder.

"Adam Story, today you're twelve years old. If you succeed in this endeavor, you will be the youngest human ever to do so. You will be famous worldwide. That's for certain. Everyone from Alaska to Australia, from Argentina to Afghanistan, will certainly know about your fabulous feat."

I stared at the laptop. Neither man nor mongoose moved.

"But the world is over twenty-six thousand miles around!" I exclaimed. "I've been no farther from home than Disneyland, and that's, like, four hundred miles from here. Mom and I drove down Interstate 5, spent six hours in the Magic Kingdom, and came straight home. That's it. I know nothing about trains or ships or whatever transportation is needed to cross continents and oceans. Besides, I don't have any money."

The man reached into his pocket again. He withdrew a blue cell phone and a GPS unit, also blue.

"MVP will supply you with all the money you need," he said. "My staff has worked out a complete bus, train, and ship schedule for you. Wherever you need to spend a night, you'll stay at a first-class hotel. Whenever you need assistance, you can press the letters M-V-P on this phone and an MVP guide will answer. It's a satellite phone that will work anywhere on earth with certainty. Furthermore, if ever you wish to quit the challenge, MVP will provide you with the quickest and safest transport home to San Francisco. That's for certain."

Prince Oh held up the other blue gadget. "You will also be carrying this GPS tracking unit. Do you know how it works?"

I nodded. I knew a lot about the Global Positioning System. Our government sent twenty-four GPS satellites into space and positioned them around the world. With a GPS unit, sailors on the ocean, pilots in the air, and hikers in the mountains can tell their exact location. I glanced at the LCD screen on the GPS that Prince Oh held.

"Right now, we're sitting at 37 degrees, 51 minutes latitude, 122 degrees, 11 minutes longitude," I recited. "And 182 meters altitude."

Prince Oh nodded. "When you carry this device, Adam Story, your location will be transmitted to MVP headquarters. We can trace you, meter by meter, anywhere you are, land or sea, with certainty."

"So what about my mom?" I asked. Not that I was considering actually going on this goofy trip. I was just curious. "Mom's not about to let me traipse across Europe and Asia by myself. She gets nervous when I walk to the mall alone."

"Your mother has scheduled three back-to-back camp sessions for you this summer," Prince Oh said.

"Oh, right," I said, remembering. "Two weeks at soccer camp, two weeks at wilderness camp, followed by twelve days at Y camp. Sounds like torture. It's as if my mom is trying to get rid of me all summer. That's forty days of camp!"

Prince Oh consulted his PDA. "The first camp session begins on July 14," he said. "If you begin your journey on that day, you'll return home on the last day of camp. MVP will make sure the camps never miss you. Your mother won't know about the grand detour until you're famous and rich."

"Rich?" I asked.

Prince Oh grinned, spreading out his two chins. "Certainly," he said. "I haven't mentioned the prize yet, Adam Story. If you become the first twelve-year-old to travel around the world, solo, crossing land and sea only, *and* you do it within the forty-day limit, MVP will reward you with four million dollars. That's for certain."

360. That's the number of our third-floor apartment. Number 360 has two small bedrooms, one moldy bathroom, and a dingy living room next to a narrow kitchen with a dripping sink and greasy walls. The front windows look out onto a parking lot. The rear of a restaurant screens sunlight from coming through the back ones. The apartment bakes in the summer, but with the restaurant smoke in the air, we rarely open the windows.

When I arrived home that day, I grabbed my large atlas, a birthday gift from Mom at breakfast. I dropped it on the living room floor and flopped it open to the world map. Displaying the world this way, on shiny double pages with crisscrossing longitude and latitude lines, made it appear small. I searched for the shortest route from the left side of the map to the right.

Placing my finger on San Francisco, I slid it across the United States until it poked New York City. From there, several routes were possible. You could cross the Atlantic, cut through Europe to Turkey, then cross some of the "stan" countries all the way to China. Or you could sail into the Mediterranean Sea, through the Suez Canal, and on to India. I studied the map some more. Maybe cutting through Africa would be faster. Or how about the northern route over Scandinavia and Russia?

My finger landed on the east coast of Asia. It made a beeline across the Pacific Ocean to California.

"That's it!" I said. "Little sweat to become world-famous and four million dollars richer."

But what was I thinking? Did I really intend to ditch summer camp and take a forty-day trip around the world? No way. I get nervous riding BART to San Francisco by myself.

"Birthday boy, quit playing with your maps and come peel potatoes," Mom called from the kitchen. She was cooking fish fingers. For dinner we tend to have the same dishes she served middle school students for

lunch that day, lots of turkey à la king, sloppy joes, corn puppies, and meat loaf surprise.

After we ate, Mom brought out a chocolate cake she'd baked at work.

"Sorry we couldn't have done more for your birthday, Adam," she said. "Money's tight, as always. I'll need to work again this summer for the cleaning service."

"The atlas and the cake are great, Mom," I said.

The cleaning service was my mother's name for going into the huge houses of my classmates to scrub their floors and squeegee their windows. The other fifth graders already looked at me as some sort of charity case, on account of Mom's job and me being able to attend their fancy school. The cleaning job made things worse.

"At least you'll have a good summer at camp, Adam," Mom said. "I want you to make friends, join in the games, and stop being such a loner. We're lucky the school district gave you grants to attend camp."

Although I never said so, the thought of camp depressed me. Being stuck with cabin mates, swimming buddies, and craft partners, and having to participate in team games, dining hall sing-alongs, and group campfires, was not my idea of fun.

I lay in bed that night, restless. Even with the window closed, whiffs of grilling steaks and frying fish filtered in from the restaurant out back.

My mind filled with thoughts of adventure. One moment I was sailing in a schooner across the seven seas. Next, I was riding in a Land Rover, searching for rhinos on the African savanna. I dreamed of hiking in the Himalayas, exploring tropical islands, skiing down snowy glaciers, and gorging on cream-filled éclairs in French cafés.

The blast of a car horn brought me back to my small, crummy world.

"No, this moldy apartment is my whole domain," I said, before drifting off to sleep. "The only way I'll ever explore the world is through the World Wide Web on a school computer. Happy twelfth birthday to me, Adam Story. This is the way life is, and this is the way it will always be."

Here is a list of places I visited on the Internet that I wished to visit for real someday:

1. Pyramids of Giza, Egypt
   (I want to climb the highest one)
2. Great Wall of China (I want to walk along the top)
3. Nile River (longest river on earth)
4. Amazon River (second-longest river on earth)
5. Grand Canyon (I want to hike to the bottom)
6. Mount Rushmore
7. Mount Everest, Nepal (highest mountain on earth)
8. The Matterhorn
   (the real one in Switzerland, not Disneyland)
9. Mount Fuji, Japan (looks cool)
10. White House, Washington, DC

11. Empire State Building, NYC
    (the movie *King Kong* is great!)
12. Taipei 101 building
    (1,667 feet, world's tallest skyscraper)
13. Sears Tower, Chicago
    (tallest building in United States)
14. Taj Mahal, India
15. South Pole
16. North Pole
17. Yellowstone National Park (see Old Faithful erupt)
18. Masai Mara Game Reserve, Kenya
19. Machu Picchu, Peru
    (ancient city in Andes Mountains)
20. Eiffel Tower, Paris
21. Disney World, Disneyland Paris, Tokyo, and Hong
    Kong (I've been to Disneyland, California)
22. Las Vegas (looks weird)
23. Venice, Italy
24. Jerusalem
25. Prime meridian, England (I want to stand on it)
26. The equator (I want to stand on it)
27. Niagara Falls, NY (looks cool)
28. Victoria Falls, Africa (world's tallest waterfall)
29. Major League Baseball stadiums
    (I want to see every one)
30. The International Space Station (who knows?)

May passed quickly. School was a total bore. Fifth-grade social studies covers American history, starting in September with Christopher Columbus. By mid-

May we hadn't yet reached the Civil War, so our teacher crammed all the stuff about slavery, the Confederacy, and the Gettysburg Address into a few weeks.

"Funny how American kids can get through fifth grade and know nothing about what happened after 1865," I told my teacher. "And they know even less about the rest of the world."

She gave me her look.

One day in After-School Club, just for fun, I planned an imaginary circle-the-earth journey on a laptop. All the train and ship timetables were available on the Net. I pretended to be a billionaire, so cost didn't matter. Here's my list:

1. San Francisco to Chicago (Amtrak train): $2\frac{1}{2}$ days
2. Chicago to New York (Amtrak train): $1\frac{1}{2}$ days
3. New York to France (cruise ship): 7 days
4. France to Moscow (train): $2\frac{1}{2}$ days
5. Moscow to Pacific (Trans-Siberian Railway): 8 days
6. Asia to San Francisco (ship): 15 days

Total: $36\frac{1}{2}$ days

"Only thirty-six and a half days to circle the world!" I said. "If the weather is good, if the trains are on time, if a war doesn't break out, I could make it home long before the forty-day deadline."

Throughout the first weeks of June, Prince Oh and the MVP challenge rarely left my mind. Then one morning my teacher called me to her desk.

"A visitor asked about you yesterday," she said.

I froze. "Was he wearing a black turban and cape?"

"No, he wore a green suit. He said he was from the school district office and he left a late birthday gift for you. He said you'll need it for a trip you're taking this summer."

My teacher handed me a blue backpack. It was the best kind, with an interior frame and lots of outside pockets. Inside one of the pockets I found a card bearing a single word:

ADVENTURE

"The pack must be for my summer camps," I told my teacher.

But I knew it wasn't. It came from the MVP producer.

A month later, on July 14, I used the backpack to pack for soccer camp. The camp bus was leaving at noon from my school parking lot. My mother would drive me there on the way to her cleaning job. When we arrived, dads and moms were hugging their sons and daughters good-bye. Behind them, a yellow school bus belched black diesel fumes.

"Love you," Mom said, kissing me on the forehead. "Don't forget, you promised to e-mail me every other day from camp."

I left the car, lugging the blue backpack. With all the people around the bus, I decided to sit at the After-

School Club picnic table until it was time to leave. A surprise awaited me there. On the table lay the blue cell phone and GPS unit from MVP. As I approached, the phone began to chirp.

I sat down at the picnic table. Prince Oh was on the cell phone when I answered it.

"Good show, Adam Story. You certainly made a bold decision."

"What decision?" I asked.

"A certain MVP challenge," said the prince. "You're about to travel around the world, Adam Story, that's for certain."

"How do you know I'm not going to camp to make lanyards all summer?" I said.

Prince Oh replied with one word: "Adventure."

Adventure. That word had been ringing in my head since my birthday. I had even looked it up in the dictionary:

ad·ven·ture noun: *an undertaking usually involving danger and unknown risks.*

Sure, the prize money would be great for Mom and me. Sure, fame would win me some respect from my classmates. But the thought of adventure—that was what tempted me to take up MVP's offer.

"Anyway, they're expecting me on the camp bus," I said into the phone.

"MVP will handle the details," said the prince.

I looked toward the parking lot. A man wearing green shorts and a green T-shirt was talking to the bus driver.

"So what if I did go on this trip?" I asked. "How would I start?"

"First, walk to the BART station. Take the train into San Francisco and alight at the Embarcadero stop. Follow the signs to the Greyhound bus terminal. Be certain to call MVP when you get there. Did you receive the blue backpack?"

"Sure. Thanks," I said.

"And I take it you're wearing the baggy blue jeans you usually wear for school and play."

"Sure. And I have on a white T-shirt, if that matters," I said. "But I left my apartment thinking I was going to camp. I didn't bring much money."

"As I explained, Adam Story, MVP will finance your entire trip, as long as you continue around the world," Prince Oh said. "Reach under the picnic table."

I placed my hand beneath the tabletop. My fingers met wads of gum, gobs of jelly, and other gross stuff before finding it, a small Baggie duct-taped to the wood. I yanked it off and checked the contents: a passport and two blue plastic cards.

"Your passport contains the visas you'll need to enter certain countries," Prince Oh explained. "One plastic card is an ATM card. It will work at any automated teller machine in the world. You may withdraw three hundred dollars' worth of local currency daily for spending

money. The PIN code is 3-2-7-8-4. That spells EARTH. The second card is an MVP credit card. This card has no spending limit."

"Ka-ching!" I said. I had never imagined having that much money. Taking the journey seemed easy. Was I really going to do it? Why not?

"During the summer the playground bell continues to ring at your school," Prince Oh went on. "The twelve o'clock lunch bell is your start signal. MVP has worked out a transportation schedule that you must be certain to keep if you're to complete the world tour in forty days. My staff has drawn up the safest route for you, one that avoids countries at war, regions experiencing outbreaks of contagious disease, and sea routes prone to tropical storms."

I panicked. Storms? Disease? War? And what about crime? And terrorists?

Prince Oh must have seen the expression on my face. "Be certain to follow MVP's chosen route and you'll be safe, Adam Story," he assured me. "Today is July 14. To win the MVP prize money, you must be back at that picnic table on August 23 before the noonday bell rings."

"But what if I get sick?" I asked. "What if the police stop me? What if I miss a connection? What if I lose the blue cards?"

This time, the reply was a dial tone.

I dropped the phone and the GPS unit into an outside pocket of my backpack. The cards went into my wallet.

When I stood, something rattled in my pants pockets.

Poker chips. Throughout fifth grade, my teacher gave us a poker chip each time we did something "positive" in class, like cleaning our desks or lining up without talking. We could cash the chips in for free time, stickers, stuff like that. At the end of the year two dozen poker chips remained in my pockets. Now the chips, along with something we had learned in social studies, gave me an idea. Pioneers had carved their names on rocks and trees along the Oregon Trail so people in the future would know they had been there. Why not announce my own presence?

"Twenty-four free-time poker chips are in my pockets," I said to myself. "And there are twenty-four time zones. I'll leave one chip in each zone. Proof that Adam Story was there."

The first poker chip I pulled out of my jeans was white. I stuck it to the gum on the underside of the picnic table.

"One for Pacific Daylight Time," I announced.

In the parking lot, campers were climbing onto the bus. Mothers and fathers still stood there, waving good-bye and blowing kisses. The man in green had left.

Riiiiiiiiiiiing!

The playground bell gave me a jolt. I hoisted the blue backpack onto my shoulders. Pressing a tiny button on my black digital watch, I set the time to the ring.

12:00 noon.

"OK, I'm off to circle the world," I said. "See you all in forty days!"

With a last look at the camp bus, I took a deep breath.
I adjusted the backpack straps and took another breath.
Then I took my first step forward.

Time Zone 1, PDT (Pacific Daylight Time)

First stop was the ATM at the Wells Fargo Bank down
the street. I inserted the blue card and pressed E-A-R-T-
H. Out spit fifteen twenty-dollar bills.

"Ka-ching!" I said. "So far so good."

BART, the Bay Area Rapid Transit, took me toward
San Francisco. Before the train ducked into the tunnel
under San Francisco Bay, the Golden Gate Bridge
appeared in the distance.

"East, east, and more east after this, bridge," I said.
"Next time I see you, I hope it'll be from the other
side."

From the Embarcadero station, the hike to the
Greyhound terminal was four blocks. Outside the
entrance I took out the cell phone and pressed M-V-P.

A woman answered. "Good afternoon, Adam. My
name is Miss J. I will be your worldwide phone guide
for the next forty days. Now, your GPS signal tells me
that you're standing at the corner of First Street and
Mission."

Weird. The MVP people could follow my every
move.

"So what do I do next, Miss J?" I asked.

"Your local time is 12:51 p.m.," the woman said. "Now

you need to catch the 1:15 bus to Chicago. Chicago is your first stop."

"Chicago, sure," I said. "I'm on my way."

"And remember, Adam, it's vital that you keep to the MVP timetable. You'll arrive in Chicago in two days, on Tuesday, at 1:40 p.m. Central Daylight Time. Call MVP as soon as you disembark. Bon voyage."

Some people might think a two-day bus trip would sound grueling. Not me. Two days to sit back and watch the United States flow by seemed great.

I entered the station and bought my ticket—no problem using the MVP credit card. With twelve minutes until the bus left, I stocked up on trip supplies at the Snack and Gift Shop. I bought a bag of Oreos, a sack of Gummi Worms, a box of Cracker Jack, a jumbo bag of M&Ms, a two-liter jug of Mountain Dew, an American Automobile Association map of the country, and four X-Men comic books.

"That should last a day," I said.

An announcement called me to Gate 3, where a bus with CHICAGO above the windshield was waiting. Still, as I mounted the bus steps, one thought nagged at me. Did I or didn't I turn off my bedroom radio before leaving the apartment?

The bus pulled out at 1:15 sharp. Minutes later it was heading east across the Bay Bridge.

"Good-bye, home! Hello, world!" I said to the whole outside.

The bus was almost full. My seat was near the front,

and I felt lucky not to have anyone sitting next to me. A man and his girlfriend, both with snake tattoos crawling up their arms, sat behind me. In the seat across the aisle, a girl who looked about fifteen had a baby beside her.

I spread the goodies on the empty seat as if for a picnic. Cookies went in one corner, candy in another, and the jug of Mountain Dew stood in the middle. The California afternoon was hot, but the air shooting from an overhead nozzle kept me cool. Perfect.

The scene outside the window was familiar. Mom and I drove this freeway, Interstate 80, to go camping at Lake Tahoe. According to the AAA map, the red, white, and blue I-80 badge signs would lead us all the way to Chicago.

After Sacramento, the bus wound into the mountains, the Sierra Nevada, with views of piney hills and twinkling lakes. Car rooftops hauling sleeping bags, suitcases, sea kayaks, surfboards, and bicycles passed under my window.

"I'm on top of the world!" I said to a passing SUV.

Around 5:00, however, the trip turned sour. The baby across the aisle started to wail. The tattooed man kept kicking my seatback, the air-conditioning quit, and my butt hurt.

Not only that, but my bladder was about to burst from all the Mountain Dew I drank. The bus had a toilet closet in the rear that smelled of chemicals, but I was too squeamish to use it.

Finally, at 6:00, the bus stopped in Reno, Nevada, for a dinner break. I leaped off and headed straight to the men's room. Nevada allows gambling, and slot machines flashed everywhere, even in the bus station, even in the restroom.

The station also had a small café, where I ordered a hamburger and fries. I sat on the curb outside and ate. The sun was sinking, and the sky looked purplish. I remembered the color from my old sixty-four-crayon Crayola box at school, Hot Magenta.

"Cawwww! Cawwww!" called a crow from a nearby pine tree.

While I was sitting there, an unfamiliar pang crawled into my gut. The cause wasn't hunger, illness, or nerves.

"I'm lonely and homesick already, bird," I admitted to the crow. "Maybe I'll call Mom on the blue phone. No, it's too soon, and she'd think something was wrong. A day is a long time when you're traveling. One day gone. Thirty-nine to go."

Time Zone 2, MDT (Mountain Daylight Time)

Before the bus left again, I resupplied myself at the station gift shop. Here's a list of the things I bought:

1. Box of chocolate doughnuts
2. King-size Hershey bar
3. Bag of Gummi Worms
4. Giant box of Cracker Jack
5. X-Men comic book
6. Two-liter jug of Mountain Dew
7. Book of puzzles
8. Pen with silver dollars printed on it
9. Inflatable pillow that wraps around your neck
10. Small flashlight that you squeeze to turn on
11. Travel pack containing a stubby toothbrush, a tiny tube of toothpaste, a small bottle of shampoo, a junior-size stick of deodorant, a miniature bar of soap, and a little packet of Kleenex
12. Blue vinyl tote bag stenciled with the words:
    Reno, Nevada
    Biggest Little City in the World

A new bus driver sat behind the large steering wheel. He wore a crisp gray uniform and looked wide awake.

I blew up my neck pillow and spread the new goodies on the seat beside me. When I pressed a button on my armrest, a spotlight lit up my stomach. Another button sent my seat leaning backward. Perfect.

The driver revved up the motor. He had closed the

door and pulled back the big gear stick when—*Bang!*
Bang!—someone beat on the side of the bus. The door
folded open, and an enormous man carrying a guitar
case climbed up the stairs. He was so wide he had to
walk sideways to get up the aisle.

Just my luck. The man stopped by my seat and asked,
"This free?"

I quickly gathered up my things and dropped them
in my lap. "Sure," I said.

When the man sat down, his bulk pressed me against
the side of the bus. He dropped his guitar case between
his knees, pinning my legs sideways.

The man held out a hand the size of my mom's oven
glove and I shook it.

"Name's Trav'lin' Man," he said.

Trav'lin' Man was as bald as an eraser and sweated a
lot. A patch of a beard covered the end of his chin.

"Story. Adam Story."

"Chicago?"

"Yeah."

"Me too. Chicago, a jazzy city. Three-sevenths
chicken, two-thirds cat, plus one-half goat. Chi...ca...go,
you see."

I nodded, but privately I groaned. To make things
worse, the woman in front of me leaned her seat far
back. That drove my knees toward my chest, smashing
the doughnuts on my stomach. It was going to be one
long night.

"So why're you goin' to Chicago?" the man asked.

Fortunately, he was the type of talker who answered his own questions.

"You're visitin' relatives, right? I play in jazz clubs. You like jazz? Suppose not. Kids rarely get jazzed about jazz."

I stared out the window into blackness. The bus appeared to be chasing the white arc that the headlights spread across the pavement.

"You travel much?" Trav'lin' Man asked. "I suppose not. Boys your age travel more in their heads. Being a jazzman, I travel a lot. I've traveled in every state in these United States. I like seein' new places, people, and all that jazz."

Trav'lin' Man's voice droned on, but I didn't mind. He was good company.

I fell asleep around midnight. The driver's announcement woke me up at 6:47 a.m.

"Salt Lake City, folks. We'll stop here for breakfast."

"Mountain Daylight Time," Trav'lin' Man told me. "Don't forget to set your watch ahead."

"Poker chip time!" I said, and I leaped off the bus. The second chip, a yellow one, went behind the first red plastic S in the SALT LAKE CITY BUS STATION sign on the front of the building.

Soon the bus was chugging through the Rocky Mountains. I did puzzles while Trav'lin' Man continued to talk.

"We just crossed the Continental Divide," he said in Wyoming. "Spit there and half of it will flow to the Pacific Ocean and half to the Atlantic. Ain't that jazzy?"

We had arrived in the real West. I had never imagined land could be so flat. A solid blue dome—Robin Egg Blue, according to my crayon box—stretched over the bus. The towns where we stopped had names straight out of movie westerns—Rawlings, Laramie, Cheyenne. In Cheyenne I saw a boy my age wearing a cowboy hat and boots.

Crossing Nebraska, I-80 sliced a straight line through the prairie. Here the land came in various shades of Crayola greens: Olive Green, Yellow-Green, Magic Mint, and Screaming Green.

Trav'lin' Man pointed to a small animal with short antlers and a white rump. "Antelope," he said.

"Home, home on the range," I sang.

We stopped for dinner in Kimball, Nebraska.

"I've had enough bus station sandwiches, coffee, and jazz," Trav'lin' Man said.

He led me to a mall across the street from the station. The place seemed familiar. Here I was a thousand miles from home, and I found the same clothing stores, same shoe stores, same music stores, and same eating places that lined California malls.

We entered a McDonald's, a replica of the one near my apartment. I ordered a Number 1 Meal Deal.

"Down the hatch," said Trav'lin' Man, holding a Big Mac to his mouth.

"And the esophagus, stomach, small intestine, and large intestine," I added.

Back on the bus, I slept restlessly. Any position I

tried was uncomfortable—slumping way down, leaning against the window, on my side, or curled in a ball. Nothing worked. I woke up in Iowa at 6:11 a.m., had breakfast in Des Moines at 7:15, and looked down upon the Mississippi River at 10:12.

"We're east of the Mighty Mississippi, Trav'lin' Man!" I said. "Old Man River, the Big Muddy, the Father of Waters."

A green sign read: CHICAGO 177 MILES.

"That's somethin' to be jazzed about," Trav'lin' Man replied. "My rear's really burnin'. Next time I'm takin' the train."

Time Zone 3, CDT (Central Daylight Time)

It was 2:23 p.m. when the bus pulled into the Chicago bus station. Trav'lin' Man and I climbed down the bus steps, rubbing our bottoms.

"Welcome to the Jazz City," Trav'lin' Man said. "Are kin comin' to pick you up? I suppose so. Good trav'lin' with you. Right now, I'm all jazzed up to find the scene here and play some *jazz*."

The ache in my belly returned as I watched my friend walk away. Inside the station, I pulled out the cell phone and pressed M-V-P.

Miss J answered, sounding her usual cheerful self. "Good afternoon, Adam. Congratulations on making it to your third time zone. MVP tracked your bus journey on the GPS. Now, we've made a reservation for you at a top Chicago hotel. You can rest up tonight before taking the bus to New York City tomorrow. A taxi will arrive shortly to take you there."

I groaned. Although a shower and a night in a soft bed sounded great, this was not good news. Three more days on a bus would be torture.

My thoughts turned to something Trav'lin' Man had mentioned. Why not take a train to New York? For the price of a first-class hotel, I could get a bed in the sleeper car. That's what I found when I plotted my make-believe round-the-world trip on the Internet.

At the information desk I asked a woman how to get to the train station. "I want to take the next train to New York City," I said.

The woman checked her computer. "The Lake Shore Limited leaves for New York at 7:00 this evening," she said. "Do you want me to make a reservation?"

"First-class sleeper," I said.

"Just yourself?"

This was a question I expected to hear often, and I had practiced an answer.

"I'm meeting my father in New York. My parents live apart. I'm one of those kids who're tossed back and forth when one of the parents gets fed up."

"I see," the woman said, tapping on her keyboard. "I've reserved a deluxe single sleeper for you on Amtrak train number forty-eight, Chicago to New York."

Slinging my backpack over one shoulder and my Reno tote bag on the other, I left the station. Forget the hotel. By taking the train, I would save time, money, and my rear end. How could MVP argue with that?

Following the woman's directions, I walked up Jefferson Street. It was good to be walking in a new city, familiar only from Internet pictures. At the corner of Jackson Boulevard, I spotted Union Station, and beyond, a building I recognized at once, the Sears Tower, the third-tallest building in the world.

It was 3:04 by my watch. The train wouldn't leave for several hours. Why not go sightseeing? I thought of my wish-to-visit list and added a mental checkmark next to the Sears Tower. After I'd hiked up Jackson Boulevard, past the train station, to the corner of Wacker Drive, the huge building towered above me. In the lobby I bought a ticket to the Skydeck on the top floor. Adults 12–64, $9.50.

"Sometimes life seems rigged," I grumbled. "When it comes to ticket prices I'm an adult. But for everything else, like movie ratings and bedtimes, I'm still a kid."

A speedy elevator shot me up to the Skydeck. What a view from up there! According to the brochure, I was looking at four states, Illinois, Indiana, Michigan, and Wisconsin. Down below, tiny Chicago cars and tiny Chicago people moved along tiny Chicago streets.

I pulled a red poker chip from my pocket. "Day 3, Time Zone 3," I said as I wedged the chip under one of the pay telescopes.

As I peered through the scope, trying to spy the Chicago Cubs baseball stadium, my cell phone chirped.

I answered it and heard Miss J's voice, serious this time. "Have you become a tourist, Adam? Why are you in the Sears Tower?"

"The hotel is out," I explained. "I'm taking the train to New York instead."

The phone went silent. After a long moment Miss J returned. "Now, what's this about taking the train tonight, Adam?"

"The train will save time. The bus is torture."

"Adam, Prince Oh explained to you that MVP made arrangements and reservations for your entire round-the-world journey. If you break the schedule, we cannot guarantee that those reservations will still be available."

"The train is already reserved," I said. "How could

getting to New York a little early screw things up?"

"Adam, *go to the hotel*," Miss J said. It sounded more like an order than advice. "Take a hot shower and get yourself a good meal. You've done an excellent job reaching Chicago. But—listen to me closely—*you are not to get on that train tonight.* Understand? Now, one of our MVP staff will meet you down in the lobby to help you get a taxi to the hotel."

"Sure," I said.

Startled by Miss J's words, I rode the elevator down to the ground floor. I recognized the MVP person immediately. He stood in the middle of the lobby with his feet spread and his hands clasped behind his back. At least seven feet tall, he wore a suit that was totally green. Jacket, shirt, and pants, down to his socks and shoes, all green.

The man glanced from side to side as I approached. "We must hurry, Adam," he said, taking my bags.

I followed the green giant out to Wacker Drive, where a yellow taxi was waiting. The MVP man told the driver where to go while I got in the back alone.

The hotel was first-class all right. After pushing through a heavy revolving door, I stood in a fancy lobby all Carnation Pink and Canary Yellow. The receptionist smiled when I walked up to the desk and dropped my bags on the floor.

"Welcome to Chicago, Mr. Story," she said. "We've put you in our Presidential Suite."

"Sweet," I said.

The suite was huge, bigger than my apartment. The main room had a white sofa, white stuffed chairs, and a white refrigerator stocked with Mountain Dew. The bedroom had a king-size bed and a king-size HDTV with a DVD and VCR player.

Instead of a shower, I took a bath in the king-size bathtub with the bubble bath that they give you free. Afterward, I put on a white, movie-star bathrobe and lay down on the sofa.

"So how do you order room service in a place like this?" I wondered.

As if on cue, a teenaged bellhop in a Brick-Red coat entered the room. A plastic nametag said he was Pip. Pip placed a large basket filled with fruit, candy, and chocolate on the coffee table.

"Compliments of MVP, Mr. Story," he said. He studied me for a moment and then asked, "Are you some sort of celebrity? I've been told to give you the VIP treatment."

"I'm just an ordinary twelve-year-old kid, traveling around the world alone," I answered.

"Well, Mr. Ordinary Kid, would you like a massage in the hotel spa?" Pip asked. He stared at my white sneakers. "Care for a shoeshine? Or how about having your hair styled at the salon?"

"No thanks. But one thing. Can I send an e-mail to my mom?"

"Jot it down, and consider it sent."

I quickly wrote on a scrap of paper:

Dear Mom,

Soccer camp is fun. I'm learning many new things, and I made a new friend. I get homesick sometimes.

Love, Adam

The bellhop read the note and grinned. "That's right, kid," he said. "No one can tell where you really are when you send e-mail."

After Pip left, I stuck a DVD into the player. I lay on the bed, popping M&Ms into my mouth, but I couldn't concentrate on the movie. Something bugged me. Why did Miss J sound so upset when I told her about the train reservation? Here MVP was paying for this fancy hotel, and they still wanted me to take a cheap, slow bus. How come?

There was more to this MVP challenge than they were telling me, I concluded.

The bedside clock said 5:30. The Lake Shore Limited train would leave in an hour and a half. I stared out the window at Lake Michigan. Why I did what I did next, I'm not sure. Maybe it was "traveler's itch" or maybe it was the guilt I felt staying in that plush place, but I got dressed in a clean T-shirt and jeans. I threw my old clothes into the blue backpack and loaded the Reno tote bag with chocolate and fruit from the basket.

Then, after a last look around the Presidential Suite, I left.

"I need to leave, sign out, or whatever it's called," I told the receptionist in the hotel lobby.

She looked surprised, almost shocked. "Is there a problem, Mr. Story? Isn't your suite satisfactory? We instructed Pip to treat you like royalty."

"No, no, everything was fine," I said. "I just decided to take the train to New York tonight."

"But you can't," the woman said. "You can't leave this hotel."

She picked up her telephone. I knew who she was calling, MVP, so I didn't wait around. Shouldering my bags, I shot through the revolving door and hurried down Jackson Street in a fast walk. Union Station was five blocks away. At the first street corner my cell phone chirped. I reached into my pocket and switched it off.

"With the GPS in my backpack, MVP can still trace me," I said. "But I don't have to talk to them."

I arrived at the train station as the large clock on the wall showed 6:10. The waiting room was about the size of a football field. The place was crowded and confusing. Corridors led in all directions. I followed signs to the Amtrak counter and bought my ticket.

"You can board now," said a man in a Midnight Blue sports coat. "The Lake Shore Limited leaves from Track 7. Have a good journey."

I still had time to buy some Mountain Dew for the twenty-hour trip. I returned to the waiting room and headed toward a food store. Near the end of the long room, someone grabbed my elbow from behind.

"Don't get on that train," a voice warned.

I spun around to find a short, thin woman standing there. She wore a green printed dress and green ribbons in her braided hair.

"That train's no good," she said. Her accent was strong—Jamaican, I guessed.

Shivers ran over me. I jerked my arm away. "Did MVP send you?"

"I'm here to help, Adam. I'll take you back to the hotel."

"No, I'm taking the Lake Shore Limited to New York," I insisted. "I don't care what MVP wants."

"That train's full of bad people, Adam," the woman said. "They pump sleeping gas into the rooms and rob you. Let me help."

The woman grabbed my arm again and tugged me toward the station exit.

"Cut it out. Let me go," I said, but without a struggle. To look like some spoiled kid trying to ditch his teacher or caretaker would have drawn attention. "Listen, if I can't take the train, tell MVP the deal's off. I'll take a plane home tonight."

At that moment the woman glanced up and released my arm. She took five steps away from me, as if I'd given off a bad smell. She looked afraid.

I glanced toward the balcony above the waiting room. Standing at the railing, holding a brass spyglass to one eye, was a man with a long gray beard. One of those loose Arab scarves covered his head. A kaffiyeh, I think

it's called. This kaffiyeh had black and white stripes like a zebra or a referee's jersey. A silver band held it on the man's head.

The instant our eyes met, the man ducked behind a pillar.

"What's going on here?" I asked the green woman. "Who was that man?"

The woman kept her distance. "We'll go back to the hotel, Adam," she said. Her eyes kept rolling toward the balcony. "Forget the train. Trust MVP. Be a good boy."

But I was more determined than ever to get on the Lake Shore Limited. Two Chicago police officers had just strolled into the waiting room. With the MVP woman watching, I walked up to them.

"Officers, I'm lost," I said. "Do you know where I can find the train to New York? It leaves at 7:00."

"You traveling alone, kid?" one officer asked.

"Yeah," I said, and repeated my divorced-parents story.

"Come on," the second officer said. "We'll take you to your train."

"Parents these days," said the first. "They expect kids to cross the country on their own. Parents aren't even parents anymore."

Flanked by the two policemen, I started toward the Amtrak corridor. I checked the balcony, but the man in the striped kaffiyeh had disappeared. The MVP woman, however, tailed us.

Upon reaching Track 7, I thanked the officers and

handed my ticket to the train attendant. I looked back as I stepped onto the first-class sleeper car. The green woman was leaning against a pole, talking on a cell phone.

Once again I wondered, Why doesn't MVP want me on this train?

The train attendant showed me to my sleeper. I entered and locked the sliding door. Outside the window the MVP woman was still on her cell phone.

"So MVP knows I'm on the train," I said. "Now what?"

I remained seated until the train pulled out of the station. Although the deluxe cabin was small, it had everything. The sofa I sat upon folded into a bed. A small sink stood in the corner, and a TV hung on the wall. I pressed a button on the little table under the window and heard music. I pressed another button, and the TV went on.

Chicago passed by like an old movie. The city had grown gray, and streetlights flashed upon the windowpane. I held my stomach. Loneliness. Homesickness.

Why not call my mother? I thought. MVP was footing the bill. I took out the phone and turned it on, but immediately I heard *Chirp! Chirp! Chirp!,* so I flipped it off.

I would call her from New York, I decided. In New York I would have many big decisions to make. Should I continue on this journey, or should I take the first jet home?

A knock rattled the door, and that rattled me.

"Ticket, please," said a voice.

I let the conductor in.

"Traveling by yourself, son?" the man asked while checking my ticket.

"Yeah. It's a long story."

"Well, that's interesting. There's another young person on this train—just two doors down—who's traveling unaccompanied. Nice girl, about your age," the conductor said. "She boarded the train in Los Angeles."

Alone again, I lowered the bed and lay down. Odd coincidence. How common was it for two twelve-year-olds to travel on the same train by themselves? Maybe the girl really was visiting a divorced parent. Still, I was curious. The episode with the green woman back in Chicago had me worried. I decided to check this girl out.

Leaving the cell phone and the GPS behind, I left the cabin. I walked down the narrow hallway, passed one door, and knocked on the next. The door was open a crack, and I could see the bed. Strange. There lay a blue backpack, the same style as mine.

The door slid open farther, and a girl with freckles stood there. She wore blue jeans, a hooded blue sweatshirt, and blue sneakers. Even her short hair was dyed blue.

"What?" she said.

"The conductor said you were traveling by yourself, like me," I said.

The girl stared at me blankly.

"Can I ask your age?" I said.

"Twelve. What of it?"

"And where's your next stop?"

"New York. Why the interview?"

"Something's weird here," I said, pointing to the blue bag on the bed. "You see, back in my cabin, I have that identical backpack. I'm taking the train to New York, too, but I'm not stopping there. I'm going to keep going, if you know what I mean."

The girl swiped her blue bangs off her brow. "How old are *you?*" she asked.

"Twelve."

"And you're attempting to...?" She revolved her pointer finger in the air.

"That's right. I'm headed home to San Francisco...*the long way.*"

"In forty days," we said together.

The girl opened the door wider. "Come in. We better talk."

I entered the compartment and sat on the bed next to the backpack. A patch was sewn on the front. It showed a space capsule with "GVP" stitched across it. Beside some travel guides on the table lay a blue cell phone and a GPS unit.

Leaving the door open, the girl sat down on the seat across from me. "I'm Meredith," she said.

"Madam, I'm Adam," I said.

The girl made a face.

"That's a palindrome," I explained. "You can write

Madam, I'm Adam forward and backward."

"Wow," said the girl.

"Hey, you just said a palindrome, too."

"I did, did I?"

We sat staring at each other in dumb silence. The chirp of her cell phone sounded like a car alarm going off. Meredith answered it while I looked out the window. Against the black outside, our reflections appeared in the glass.

"Hello?... Oh, hi... Yes, I'm in my cabin. Everything's OK."

I held my finger to my lips.

"Yes, I'm alone... No, I haven't left the room yet... Fine, sure I will."

Meredith hung up and shook her head.

"I'm not to leave this sleeper," she said. "All my meals will be delivered here."

"MVP tried to stop me from getting on this train," I explained. "They didn't want us to meet."

"MVP?" Meredith asked.

"That's my team, the Magellan Voyage Project."

"A guide from GVP, *my* team, was on the phone," Meredith said. "That stands for the Gagarin Voyage Project."

"Yuri Gagarin, the Russian, the first man to orbit the earth in space," I said.

Meredith nodded. "Two teams. Two twelve-year-olds. What's going on?"

"I have no idea."

For the next twenty minutes I told Meredith about my mother, our crummy apartment, and how I was supposed to be at camp all summer. I explained how Prince Oh made me the around-the-world-in-forty-days challenge.

"My parents think I'm visiting my grandma in Cleveland for six weeks," Meredith said. "My mom is a flag lady for a highway work crew. My dad paints the white stripes down the center of the highway. They fight a lot. Home is never happy, and since we move so much, no place is home for long. That's why when GVP offered me the chance to travel, I jumped at it."

"Who made you the challenge?" I asked.

"Her name's Queen Mumumu, last survivor of a Polynesian dynasty."

"Did she mention something called the League of Royalty without Domains?"

"LORD? Right, Queen Mumumu's ancestors once ruled an island in the South Pacific. But centuries ago a volcano erupted on the island and the entire kingdom sank."

"And when did you start this trip?" I asked.

"July 14 at noon. GVP told me to wear something blue."

"It all fits," I said. "I remember Prince Oh's exact words before I left California. He said the prize would go to the *first* twelve-year-old to travel around the world alone. He never mentioned that another twelve-year-old would be starting out at the same time."

"So this is a race?" Meredith said.

I nodded. "Seems like it. Some crazy race."

"Between MVP and GVP?"

"Between you and me, two kids who don't mind being away from home for a few weeks."

Meredith studied a train schedule on the table. "Well, I quit," she said. "The train arrives in Cleveland late tonight, and I do have a grandmother there. This around-the-world *race* sounds creepy, too dishonest. If our royal producers lied about the race, maybe they lied about the prize money, too."

I returned to my cabin but couldn't sleep. I lay in my

bed, thinking. Prince Oh hadn't told me everything, and there was more to learn. Who was the woman in green? Who was the man in the striped kaffiyeh?

At 3:00 a.m. the train stopped in Cleveland, Ohio. I looked out the window. Meredith was standing on the platform with her blue backpack.

"Has she really decided to quit the race and end her voyage here?" I asked myself. "Or did her GVP team give her new instructions on the phone?"

The train pulled away from the platform. Meredith's blue hair fluttered in its windy wake.

Time Zone 4, EDT (Eastern Daylight Time)

At 3:02 the following afternoon, the train arrived at Pennsylvania Station in New York City.

"Day 6," I said, stepping down to the platform.

Lugging my blue backpack and Reno tote bag, I started for the lobby.

I had done a lot of thinking the night before. The MVP ATM card and credit card remained in my pocket. I could find a hotel and stay in the Big Apple a few days. Or, if I wanted, I could catch a plane and be home in six hours. First, though, I wanted to call MVP. I needed to tell Prince Oh that I was steamed. He had misled me. I pulled out my blue cell phone and pressed M-V-P.

Miss J answered. "Adam, we're glad you are safe." She sounded calm.

"Let me talk to His Majesty, Prince Oh," I said. "I

know about the race. I know I'm not alone in the challenge. There's a girl named Meredith who was also going around the world."

"Prince Oh is unavailable at this hour, Adam," Miss J said. "Now, what would you like to do? There's a 4:45 flight to San Francisco. We could have a driver take you to the airport, and you could be at camp in time for tonight's campfire."

This was not what I expected. Miss J wasn't rattled at all about my discovery. She didn't seem to care if I continued the race or not.

"What would I do if I decided not to quit?" I asked.

"The next leg on your world tour would take you across the Atlantic Ocean. MVP has made a first-class reservation for you on the *Queen Mary 2*. It sails tomorrow morning for England."

"The *QM2!*" I said so loudly that two women in the station turned to glare at me.

The *Queen Mary 2* was the largest, longest, tallest, and most luxurious ocean liner in the world. I'd visited its web site. It looked like a palace.

"And if you don't like England, you can fly home, first-class, on the first flight back to San Francisco," the guide said.

My anger was evaporating fast.

"What would I do if I stayed in New York?" I asked.

"For now you can take a cab to your hotel, The Plaza. MVP has reserved a very nice room for you there."

I also knew The Plaza. That's where Eloise lived.

My mom read me the *Eloise* picture books when I was little.

"Sounds mawvelous," I said.

A night at The Plaza and a transatlantic cruise on the *QM2* sounded too good to pass up. It sure beat being eaten by mosquitoes at camp. Even if the MVP challenge was a race, it was a first-rate one.

When I turned around, a frowning Japanese man built like a sumo wrestler stood there. He wore the same green suit as the MVP man in Chicago. Without a word he led me outside to a taxi.

My hotel room was even fancier than the one in Chicago. The bed could have slept five fifth graders. My entire class could have had a great party in the living room. Bottles of Mountain Dew filled the refrigerator, and bowls of M&Ms and Gummi Bears waited on every table, counter, and shelf.

After a quick shower I called home.

"Adam, I can't believe you called," my mother said. "How's camp? I got your e-mail and letter. An actual snail-mail letter! What a surprise!"

My mind whirled. MVP must have sent Mom a phony camp letter to cover me.

"Soccer camp's great," I said. "I'm getting lots of exercise." I looked out the window at Central Park. "And there are loads of trees here and a lake."

"I'm so glad you made a friend, Adam," Mom said. "I worry about you spending so much time alone."

Soon after we said good-bye, Miss J called.

"Now, Adam, you have all afternoon to relax in your room," she said. "But MVP insists that you remain in the hotel. I'll call later with instructions for boarding the QM2. OK?"

I threw the cell phone onto my bed.

"Being in New York City without seeing New York City is not OK," I said. "I'll just make sure MVP can't find me."

After placing my GPS in front of the TV, I left the room. Instead of taking the elevator, I raced down the stairs to the lobby. On the ground floor I opened the door a crack. The green sumo wrestler stood by the reception desk. MVP must have posted him there to guard me.

"Sorry, team," I said. "I prefer being on my own."

By taking a side exit I escaped the green man's notice. Soon I was out on the streets of New York. This was great. On almost every block I saw a familiar sight.

Here's a list of things I recognized in the Big Apple:

1. Rockefeller Center and the ice-skating rink
2. The stone lions in front of the main library
   (I wedged a blue poker chip behind the lion
   on the right-hand side)
3. Empire State Building (another check for
   my wish-to-visit list)
4. Macy's department store (I watch the giant-balloon
   parade every Thanksgiving)
5. Broadway (Mom loves Broadway musicals)
6. Times Square (where the ball drops on New Year's
   Eve—last year my mom let me stay up to watch)

My legs were sore by the time I reached Times Square. As I sat on a bench to rest, a yellow taxi pulled up to the curb. The green MVP man stepped out of the back seat and stood by the cab. He said nothing, but I knew what he was telling me.

MVP was hard to trick. Their eyes were everywhere. Maybe something on me even contained a tracing chip.

I stood and walked toward the cab. The sumo wrestler nodded as I dove into the back seat.

"The Plaza," I told the driver.

Time Zones 5, 6, 7, 8

I awoke with a bad headache and a growling stomach.

"Where am I?" I groaned.

The entire room, ceiling, walls, and floor, seemed to sway. Could I be back home in California? Earthquake country!

I rolled out of bed and staggered to the window. From horizon to horizon I saw nothing but choppy ocean, Aquamarine.

"I'm aboard the *QM2*," I said. "I'm somewhere on the Atlantic Ocean."

My stomach gurgled, telling me I hadn't eaten in a long time. I searched the cabin and discovered a basket full of fruit and candy on the dresser. A card taped to the handle read:

Adam,

    Bon voyage while crossing your 5th, 6th, 7th, and 8th time zones! Keep up the good work. We're proud of you. Remember, we're just a phone call away.

                    Your MVP team

I shoveled handfuls of M&Ms in my mouth and chomped on an apple. As I ate, I noticed my blue back-pack lying on the floor. A wooden dart stuck out of its side. My throbbing brain started to remember things.

On July 20, Day 7 of my journey, I'd woken up early at The Plaza. MVP called and told me to take a taxi to the Passenger Ship Terminal. My ticket for the *QM2* was waiting at the reception desk when I checked out.

I arrived at the terminal and checked in. All one thousand one hundred gleaming black and white feet of the *Queen Mary 2* towered above the pier. A crowd of people stood on the dock, waving to people already on board. The scene was thrilling, lots of cheering and confetti fluttering in the air. Passengers tossed streamers from ship to shore, just like in the movies.

I stepped onto the gangway. Halfway up the ramp it happened. Something stung my left leg. Looking down, I found a three-inch dart piercing my jeans. The dart, a wooden missile with colorful feathers at the end, stuck out below my thigh.

"Yeow!" I cried.

I pulled out the dart and put it in my pocket. Peering over the side of the gangway, I saw something bizarre, even for New York. In a far dark corner of the pier crouched a teenaged boy. He wore red sweatpants and a red sweatshirt with the hood pulled up. A large white "79" appeared on his back. Against his lips he held a long tube that could be only one thing, a blowgun.

By now, my head was swimming. I saw two of everything—two crouching men, two crowds of well-wishers, two *Queen Mary 2* names painted on the bow of the ship.

I staggered up the double ramp. At the ship's entrance, a woman greeted me.

"Are you all right?" she asked with slow, slurred words.

"Madam, I'm Adam," I said, handing over my ticket. "MVP VIP."

"I'll show you to your stateroom, Mr. Story," the steward said.

Dizzy, I followed her down a corridor. My eyelids felt like sacks of sand. A line of spit dribbled from my lower lip. We stopped before a door and I stumbled into a large room. The instant the woman left, I dropped onto the bed. The blast of the ship's horn was part of my dream.

Now, so many hours and miles later, I looked out the window again. I didn't even remember the *QM2* leaving New York harbor.

I pulled out the feathered dart that was stuck in the side of my backpack, and I took the first one out of my pocket. The tips must have had a tranquilizer on them, some sort of sleeping drug. How long was I out?

I found my GPS and switched it on. The screen read:

36°16′latitude, 58°22′longitude

According to a map on the wall, the ocean liner was over a fifth of the way from New York to England. I pressed a button, and the date and time appeared:

July 8, 6:43

"I've been asleep for an entire day," I said. "No wonder I'm starving."

At that moment the phone chirped, and I answered it.

"Adam, are you all right?" Miss J said. "Why haven't you answered the phone for the past twenty-four hours? Why haven't you left your cabin?"

"I've been asleep," I said. "Someone shot sleeping darts at me."

"Sleeping darts? Are you sure?"

"Sure, I'm sure. I'm holding them."

"You've been shot?" Miss J exclaimed. "How is this possible?"

"I saw this guy with a four-foot blowgun just before

I passed out. He looked about eighteen, dressed in red sweats with '79' on the back."

The phone went dead. A minute later Miss J's voice returned, sounding ultra-serious. "Adam, this concerns us very much. MVP doesn't know who's responsible. We feel, however, that you'll be safe aboard the ship until it arrives in England in five days."

"Good to know," I said, rubbing my aching head.

"An MVP staff member will meet you at Southampton, where the *QM2* docks. You may need to abort your mission there. From now on, it's critical that you follow all our instructions."

"Maybe I want to fly straight back to the United States," I said.

"That is your option," Miss J said. "But no matter your choice, be extremely careful once you set foot in Europe. Trust no one. Make sure all MVP personnel show you MVP ID. You're important to us, Adam."

The next five days passed peacefully. With no green-clad people, men in striped kaffiyehs, or teenagers with blowguns on board, the days were uneventful as well. I swam in the five pools, took my pick of the ten restaurants, exercised in the spa, watched movies in the cinema, visited the planetarium, and surfed the Net in the computer room.

Two or three times Mom and I exchanged e-mail. I enjoyed making up soccer camp stories. If she only knew my e-mail really came from the middle of the Atlantic Ocean.

On Thursday morning, July 25, the ship's captain made an announcement: "Attention, passengers, if you look out the port side of the ship, you'll spot the southern coast of England."

I stood at the railing. On the horizon lay a dark pink line, Wild Strawberry.

"Europe," I told myself. "Second continent. Day 12."

Part II
Europe

"Home is where you can call the bed your own."

Time Zone 9, BST (British Summer Time)

Most of the *QM2* passengers walked down the gangway relaxed and in good spirits. I stepped down frightened and lonely.

In the arrival area, a blond woman wearing a green pantsuit barged through the crowd toward me. She held up a card as if she were an FBI agent. The card bore the MVP logo with some words underneath:

"The darts, Adam. Do you have them?" she asked with a Scandinavian accent.

"Sure," I said, and handed over the two feathered stingers.

"Prince Oh sends his sincere apologies about this disturbance in your journey," the woman said. "It was a gross violation of game rules. Game referees will conduct a full investigation."

"Game?" I asked. "What game? I thought I was in a race. What game?"

"You'll meet with Prince Oh in Paris tonight," the woman said. "Our producer thought it best to delay telling you the details of the Great Global Game until it was necessary. That time has come."

"Great Global Game? Who's playing this game? Who made the rules?"

"Adam, you've managed to reach your ninth time zone in twelve days. Among LORD members the betting ran one hundred to one against your making it this far. The whole MVP team is very proud of your accomplishment, but you must be patient. Game Rule 81 states that a producer can meet with a player for only one hour in the forty-day period. We must use that hour wisely."

"What's a player?" I asked. "What's a pilot?"

"Pilots, such as myself, are team members who assist players, help them buy tickets, find the correct trains, or pass through customs safely," the woman explained. "You, Adam, are the MVP player in the GGG. You must wait a few hours for the other answers. You'll be taking the Eurostar to France. We know how interested you are in that train."

That was true. I knew a lot about the Chunnel, the train that speeds through a tunnel under the English Channel. London to Paris in two and a half hours.

"Game Rule 25 states that a pilot can remain with a player for only ten minutes," the MVP woman said. "We must hurry. Most likely, a referee is watching us."

Taking my arm, the pilot rushed me to a train waiting near the dock. She parted with these instructions. "This train will take you to Waterloo Station in London. That's where the Eurostar also departs for Paris. You will have a three-hour layover, but do not leave the station. Do not talk with anyone on either train. At the station, keep to crowded, well-lit areas. As soon as you reach Paris, call MVP for further directions."

"Whatever you say, pilot," I said. "I'll see England, I'll see France. I hope no one sees my underpants."

The train trip to London took ninety minutes. The English countryside could have passed for Northern California with all the oak trees, grass fields, and rolling hills, Spring Green.

When I arrived at Waterloo Station, I collected my first-class ticket to Paris.

"Simple enough," I said. "But now there are three hours to fill or kill."

Across from the international ticket counter, a sign read:

Below the sign, an escalator carried people down to the subway, called the Tube. I studied the map next to the entrance. One station caught my interest, GREENWICH, pronounced with a short E and without the W.

"That's where they marked the prime meridian, zero degrees longitude, starting point for all the world's time zones," I told myself. "Now's my chance! I'm going to stand on the prime meridian whether MVP likes it or not. Another check for my wish-to-visit list!"

After I withdrew money, called pounds, from an ATM, a man at the Underground ticket booth gave me directions to Greenwich station. I descended into the Tube, and a few rides later I was there. Once I got back up to ground level, I followed signs toward the Royal Observatory.

At the corner, I started to cross the street.

Phoom!

A red double-decker bus almost mowed me down from behind. Leaping back to the curb, I remembered. In England, for some reason, they drive on the opposite side of the road.

"Travel is confusing at times," I recalled Trav'lin' Man telling me. "Daydreaming can be dangerous."

The old Royal Observatory stood on top of a grassy hill. I entered a courtyard and saw what I came to see, a long steel strip embedded in the bricks. It marked

the prime meridian, the line separating the Eastern Hemisphere from the Western Hemisphere. When the guard turned his back, I knelt down and inserted a red poker chip next to the metal band.

"Smack on zero degrees longitude," I said, standing on the line as if it were a balance beam. "Greenwich Mean Time! In the meantime, east is east and west is west, and in between I now do rest."

Reversing my Tube route, I returned to Waterloo Station. The Chunnel train was about to leave, and I found my seat in the first-class car, next to the window. Just before it took off, a woman sat beside me. She wore a long yellow dress and a yellow scarf around her head.

"Ever been to Paris before?" she asked.

"First time," I said. She was very pretty, and made me blush.

"Ah, you're an American."

"How'd you know?"

The woman smiled. "Americans never think they have an accent."

An hour after leaving London, I rose to use the restroom at the end of the car. The WC or water closet, as Europeans call it, was occupied, so I waited outside. When the door opened, a gray-bearded man came out and bumped into me. We met eyeball to eyeball. The striped kaffiyeh he wore brushed my face.

"Hi! Hey, wait!" I said.

But the man slipped by me and disappeared into the next car.

Back at my seat, I asked the woman in the yellow dress, "Did you see that man with the beard? He wore a striped headscarf. I saw someone just like him in Chicago."

The woman shook her head. "I saw no such man," she said.

At that instant the car went black. The train had entered the tunnel under the English Channel. For several seconds I could see nothing. When the lights came on, the woman next to me had disappeared.

Ninety minutes later, the train pulled into the Gare du Nord station in Paris. That's when I reached into my back pocket and discovered that my wallet was gone—money, cards, everything! Good thing my passport was still there. I pulled my blue backpack from the overhead rack and checked the pockets. The cell phone and the GPS unit were also missing.

"Just great," I said. "I'm alone in Paris, France. I don't have money to buy food or get a place to sleep. I don't even have a way to call MVP for help. Adam Story, so much for adventure. You've reached the end of your journey."

Time Zone 10, CEST (Central European Summer Time)

Should I stay in the Gare du Nord or leave? If I left, how would MVP find me? If I stayed, would the wrong people find me—teenagers with giant peashooters, perhaps?

Trust no one, Miss J had told me.

"Should I even trust Prince Oh?" I asked myself. "I'll leave the station and check out the city. See what happens."

Shouldering my backpack and tote bag, I stepped into the early evening light of Paris. I followed a wide street, not knowing where it led.

So this was France. The first thing that hit me was that people were speaking French. While walking down the crowded sidewalk, I panicked, not being able to read the signs or understand a word I heard. How would I ask questions? How would I get directions?

Dog poop! That was my next thought. Piles of dog poop lay all over the Paris sidewalks. On every block I had to swerve around at least a dozen smelly turds.

After walking about a mile, I passed the Louvre Museum. In the distance I saw the Arc de Triomphe. Finally I came to the famous river that split Paris in two, the Seine. To the left, Notre Dame Cathedral, a familiar web site sight, loomed above the trees. To the right rose the Eiffel Tower.

"Check," I said, thinking of my list.

A long walk along the riverbank took me to the pointed iron structure. I arrived there after sunset. Golden floodlights had just gone on to light up the tower like a giant birthday candle. You had to pay to take the elevator to the top, so I sat on a bench and stared upward.

While I sat there, a large van, Laser Lemon in color, drove up and parked not twenty yards from my bench.

I recognized the word stenciled on the side:

CRÊPES

A man dressed in a yellow turtleneck and yellow pants climbed from the driver's seat. His blond hair dangled below a yellow beret. He folded open the side of the van and propped it up with a stick. A string of yellow lights came on along the top edge of the van, making it look like something from a carnival midway.

Inside the van, a blond woman stood behind a counter. She too wore a yellow turtleneck, pants, and beret. I watched her pour thin batter onto a round iron griddle. She spread the batter with a wooden squeegee-like thing, waited a few seconds, flipped the skinny pancake, and squirted jelly in the center. After folding it into a triangle, she served it to a waiting tourist.

A whiff of the hot crêpe made my stomach gurgle. This reminded me of my lack of money, which reminded me of my pockets, which reminded me of the poker chips.

"New time zone," I said. "And here's the perfect spot to leave a chip."

Hoisting my backpack onto my shoulders, I stood and began burying a blue chip beside the Eiffel Tower's north leg.

As I worked, the yellow man from the crêpe van called out in a thick English accent, "Oi! 'Old on there, mate. What do you 'ave there?" He now stood inside the van, grating cheese.

"Nothing," I answered.

"Didn't look like nothing," said the woman, who spoke with a French accent and was grilling a second crêpe. "Who are you with?"

"No one," I said.

I dropped the chip in a hole, kicked dirt over it, and started to walk away.

"Oi! Where're you 'eaded, mate?" the man called out.

"Nowhere," I replied.

"*Mon dieu!* Doing nothing? With no one? Going nowhere?" the woman said. "And I suppose you are nobody."

I pulled my backpack straps with my thumbs. "None of your business," I said.

"Well, Nobody, me name's Tod," the man said. "And this is me twin sister, Dot."

I walked up to the counter. "Twins? How come you talk so differently?"

"I was raised in France, and my brother was raised in England," Dot said. "Same blood, different upbringing."

"Care for a cheese and 'am crêpe, mate?" Tod asked.

The smell was torture, but I had to shake my head. "I'm broke," I said. "No money."

The twins looked at me sympathetically. Their faces were remarkably similar.

My gurgling stomach made Dot ask, "Have you eaten dinner yet, Nobody?"

"I'm OK."

"Tell you what, mate," said Tod. "We could use some 'elp in 'ere."

"*Oui! Bien!*" said Dot. "You can slice and dice in exchange for a nice crêpe."

"Sure. Great. Deal," I said, swinging off my pack.

I entered the yellow van through a door in the back. Tod handed me a knife and I began chopping mushrooms.

"Tod and Dot, I can trust you, right?" I asked. "Well, my name's not Nobody. It's Adam Story."

"An excellent name," said Dot, who was wiping off the round griddle.

"Adam was the first somebody," said Tod as he stepped out of the van. "Back in a jiff."

I should have become suspicious when Dot also left, but my mind was on food. Seconds after I was alone, the side window slammed shut. The back door locked, and the van's engine revved.

A heavy wire screen, like one of those dog barriers in cars, separated me from the driver's compartment. I could only see the backs of Tod's and Dot's yellow berets.

"Hey! What's going on?" I shouted. "I feel like a prisoner back here."

"'Old on, mate," Tod said. "You're not a prisoner. According to Game Rule 95, you are a *detainee*."

I jolted. "Game rule? You're part of the Great Global Game?"

Both blond heads nodded.

"And capturing the MVP player will be worth a sizable tracker's fee for us," said Dot. "*Ooh la la!*"

In the front of the van, the twins shook hands.

"'Ip, 'ip, 'urrah, Dotty!" Tod said. "The perfect capture. MVP pilots 'aven't a clue where to find their player."

"*Très bien,* Tod," said Dot. "A game referee was even standing in the bushes, less than ten feet way. Our tracker's fee is guaranteed."

The van started to move and I sat down. With no windows in the back, my only view was past the heads and out the windshield. Streetlights shone upon a four-lane highway. Although the road could have been outside any large city in the world, I knew we were still near Paris.

"Where are you taking me?" I called forward.

Dot turned. "Relax, Nobody, and enjoy the crêpe I made for you back there. There'll be a three-day delay in your world tour. You've been caught by the three trickiest trackers in the entire Great Global Game."

"Three?" I asked.

The blond woman held up my wallet, cell phone, and GPS unit. "You met Tot on the Chunnel train. Of course, we removed the tracking chips."

"'Ave no fear, Nobody," said Tod. "Game rules protect players from getting 'armed. Game Rule 69 bars trackers from using traps and snares. Rule 70 bans shackles, instruments of torture, and weapons. I bet a ref would 'ave me 'ead for 'olding your 'and."

"Game rules! Game referees!" I called out. "Will someone please tell me what this Great Goofy Game is all about? Who's playing it?"

"Your producer 'as kept you in the dark, 'asn't 'e, mate?" said Tod.

"The goal of the Great Global Game is simple," said Dot. "First team player who circles the world within the forty-day deadline is the winner."

"And there are two teams?" I asked. "MVP and GVP?"

"*Non, non*, Nobody," said Dot. "Twenty-four."

"Twenty-four teams!" I exclaimed. "Like in two dozen?"

Tod and Dot nodded.

"And every team has a producer, pilots, and a twelve-year-old player?" I asked.

The blond heads nodded again.

"And what do trackers do?"

"A tracker's job is to capture players and escort them to the closest detention center," said Dot.

"Each time zone 'as a DC," said Tod. "Players are 'eld there for a seventy-two-hour penalty."

I thought of Meredith's blue hair and our blue backpacks. "So players must wear blue," I guessed. "Producers wear black, pilots green, and trackers yellow. Do referees wear striped kaffiyehs?"

"*Oui*, the one hundred GGG referees belong to a tribe of desert nomads," said Dot. "For these forty days, they're roaming the world, making sure all twenty-four teams play according to the one hundred and one game rules."

"So what team do you two belong to?" I asked.

"TVP, the Triton Voyage Project," said Dot. "Our producer is Baron Gunter von Sheepsbottom. You'll meet him shortly."

"'Is 'ighness is flying 'ere just to say 'ello," said Tod.

"Triton," I said. "Wasn't that the first submarine to travel around the world under water?"

"*Bon*, Nobody," said Dot. "You're a clever player. The baron will be thankful to have you out of the competition for three days."

I found a fork and stabbed the crêpe on the counter. The Great Global Game was much bigger than I imagined. I saw it as a giant worldwide version of Capture the Flag, Tag, and Red Rover rolled into one.

"By the way, Dot and Tod," I said, "a teenager in red sweats shot a sleeping dart at me in New York. What does it say in the Great Goopy Game rule book about that?"

The twins exchanged looks.

"'Orrible," Tod said. "Game Rule 71 forbids any drug use to capture players."

"Trackers might use sneaky tactics, but nothing that extreme," said Dot. "A referee would expel an entire team if they were caught using tranquilizers."

An hour later the van left the freeway and rattled along a gravel road that cut through a field of tall sunflowers. For miles, the headlights lit up yellow sunflower blooms, each one bowing toward the western sky.

The road ended at a large stone mansion—a château, as the French call it. We parked before four stone columns that supported the entranceway. Behind the pillars, a pair of tall glass doors opened in the middle, and out marched two huge men with bushy brown beards. Each wore an orange jumpsuit and had a ring of keys hanging from his belt.

"Oi, mates! TVP trackers 'ere to 'and over the MVP player," Tod called from the van. "'E's in good condition, but could use a 'earty meal."

"*Voilà!* Welcome to the +1 Detention Center, Nobody," Dot said to me. "The orange gentlemen will be your hosts for the next seventy-two hours."

The two orange guards, one in front, one behind, led me into the château. Dragging my bags along the polished floor, I passed through large rooms decorated as if for a museum. Golden upholstered chairs stood against golden walls under golden-framed paintings of grumpy-looking people. My footsteps echoed against the tall gilded ceiling, decorated with white clouds and naked cupids.

Our procession stopped by a bookshelf. The front guard pulled out a book. The shelf slid aside, revealing a narrow, dank corridor lit by a dim, bare light bulb. Cobwebs connected the corners. Cockroaches scurried up the clammy walls as we marched along the cold stone floor.

"You guys aren't taking me to a dungeon, are you?" I asked. "Remember, this is just a game. Right? No rough stuff. That's one of the game rules. Remember? Don't forget the rules or I'll tell one of the striped referee guys. Let's play fair. That's what teachers tell us at school."

The lead guard stopped at a large wooden door with rusty iron hinges. He turned and said something to the other in a language full of grunts and snorts.

"Great," I grumbled. "Neither of you understood a word I said, right?"

The guard unlocked the door and pushed it open. To my relief, I entered a bright, clean rec room. A quick scan showed me easy chairs, a flat-screen TV, computers, a Ping-Pong table, a pool table, and lots of flashing pinball machines. Off to the side was a small dormitory with a washroom. The large windows looked onto a swimming pool and a tennis court with the sunflower field beyond.

I tossed my luggage on a chair. "Maybe a seventy-two-hour detention won't be so bad after all," I said.

Laid out on a nearby table was enough food to please any twelve-year-old. For the next twenty minutes I gorged on six tacos, three slices of pizza, and two hot dogs. I wolfed down a cream puff and three chocolate doughnuts.

As I reached for a chicken drumstick, a sound came from the dorm room. Someone was crying. Surprised that I wasn't alone, I walked to the doorway. The dorm had four bunk beds, and on the bottom of one lay a boy with red hair. His eyes were red and his cheeks blotchy. Snot flowed out of both nostrils and formed an "11" on his upper lip.

"Hello, fellow player detainee," I called out, noting the boy's blue jeans and a blue T-shirt. "Trackers got you, too?"

The boy wiped his nose with the back of his hand.

"Who are you?" he sobbed.

"Adam Story. Magellan Voyage Project. San Francisco, California."

"My name's Pickles, Pickles Goodhaven," the boy said. "I'm from the DVP team, the Drake Voyage Project. Coo! You've come all the way from San Francisco? That's ten time zones from here!"

I nodded modestly.

"Coo! I started in Scotland," said Pickles. "Trackers caught me as I entered my second time zone."

"Tough luck," I said. "How much detention time do you have left?"

Pickles started sniveling again. Another "11" appeared below his nose. "I don't care. I just want to go home. I miss my bedroom. I miss my own bed. I'm going home tonight."

"You're quitting the game already?" I asked.

"Coo! I hate sleeping on buses and trains. I hate eating strange food and meeting strange people. I'm heading home and won't leave again for the rest of my life."

—

As we talked, a loud *Whump! Whump! Whump!* came from outside the window. A black helicopter had landed on the floodlit tennis court. The emblem on its side showed a submarine with "TVP" printed across it.

A short time later, the two guards led a tall, slender man with bushy black eyebrows into the rec room. He wore a black beret, a black turtleneck, black cargo shorts, and shiny black hiking boots with black knee socks. A square black mustache, one inch by one inch, appeared to have sprouted from his nostrils. With his skinny legs, he looked like a tall, black shore bird.

"Greeting, preteen detainees, tween travelers, adolescent adventurers," the man said to Pickles and me. "Baron Gunter von Sheepsbottom, Esquire, at your service. I'm the TVP producer, and I do hope you're enjoying your stay at +1 Detention Center."

Pickles leaped off his bunk. "Take me home!" he

wailed. "I want to go back to my own bed! My own bathtub! My own TV!"

The baron nodded sympathetically. "And so you shall, Pickles, my boy," he said. "Game Rule 30 states that any player can return home immediately upon request. Homesickness is nothing to be ashamed of, Pickles. In fact, I'll call your producer, Sheik Kaput, at once and tell him that I'll take you home to the Highlands myself. By bedtime you'll be back in your own cozy bed, with your head on your own special pillow, snug under your own comfy covers."

"Coo!" went Pickles, and he began packing his blue backpack.

Baron von Sheepsbottom turned toward me. He raised one bushy eyebrow and stroked his pointy chin with a thumb and finger. "And how about you, Mr. Story?" he said. "Would you like to go home as well? Familiar bed, familiar voices, familiar meals. You could be back at San Francisco Bay by morning."

"Sorry, baron, this place seems as good as any to spend three days," I said. "So far the Great Goony Game has been rather fun."

A thin U of a smile spread across the baron's face. "Yes, and you've made excellent progress, Mr. Story," he said. "Despite your producer not even telling you it *was* a game. Eh? Quite a scoundrel, that Prince Oh. So unfair."

I shrugged. "Who knows, maybe not knowing about the teams and all the rules was helpful," I said. "I'm not big on teams and rules."

Baron von Sheepsbottom placed a hand on my shoulder. "But unfortunately for you, Mr. Story, my TVP player, Chukudifu, is halfway across his ninth time zone already. My boy is a scrappy traveler from West Africa who decided to travel clockwise around the globe. So far he hasn't had one delay. He's smart. He's bold. He's daring. Nothing shakes him. My Chukudifu leads the GGG pack, and the pack grows thinner every day."

"I'm still in this game, baron," I said. "I'm still a player."

"I'm afraid, Mr. Story, when you're finally released from this detention center in sixty-four hours and twenty-eight minutes, you won't have the teensy-weensiest chance of winning the Great Global Game. All your effort, cunning, and hardship will be for naught. Continue in this game, Mr. Story, and you'll return home as penniless and unpopular as you were when you left. However..."

Here the baron leaned forward and whispered in my ear, "If you return home tonight, perhaps I could make a considerable private contribution to your mother's bank account."

I pulled away from the producer. "You mean, like, a bribe," I said. "I bet one of those one hundred and one game rules outlaws bribing a rival player."

Baron von Sheepsbottom's grin turned to a sneer. His postage-stamp mustache quivered. "Go home, Mr. Story," he snarled. "The game is full of silly rules. And as any schoolchild knows, rules are for bending. And if rules bend too far, they break. And broken rules are easy to hide. I swear by my ancestors' mustaches, Mr. Story, TVP will triumph in the Great Global Game, no matter how many rules need to be bent, broken, and hidden."

A shiver ran over my skin. Not for the first time I wondered why these rich royals were playing the world-wide game. For the sport? For the betting? After hearing the baron's chilling resolve to win, I knew there was more to it.

At that moment an orange guard returned to the room. He whispered something to the baron that brought a smile back to his face.

"Excellent news!" the baron said to me. "The playing field has grown smaller still. One more game contestant, Queen Mumumu's player from GVP, has been captured and will arrive at this detention center shortly."

I fell back on the bunk. "Meredith," I said under my breath.

"Day 13," I groaned, rolling from my bunk the next morning.

Pickles's bunk was empty. In the next bed, a mop of blue hair rested on the pillow.

"Small world, Meredith," I said to the sleeping form. "Trackers must have brought you in late last night."

I sniffed my armpits and decided to take a shower. After grabbing a clean T-shirt from my backpack, I went into the washroom.

When I came out, Meredith was sitting up in bed.

"Oh, no, Don Ho!" she called out.

"I suppose you knew all along we were players in some big intercontinental contest," I said.

Meredith climbed down from the bunk. She wore the same blue clothes she had on when I last saw her in Cleveland.

"I joined the GGG to win, Adam," she said. "Just because you were blank about the whole thing didn't mean I should fill you in."

I scrubbed my hair with a towel. "So what happened after Cleveland?" I asked. "How'd you end up here?"

"I took a bus to Boston. From there I sailed to Spain on a schooner. Right before we set sail, two trackers joined the crew. I should have suspected the yellow slickers they wore. When we got to Spain they offered me a lift to Paris, but they ended up driving me to this DC instead. How'd you get caught?"

"I was taken in by a crêpe," I said. "Are you heading home to LA or serving your detention time?"

Meredith said nothing, but the answer was obvious. I should have guessed back in America that she wasn't a quitter.

"Do you know what happens to game players after they're released from a detention center?" I asked.

"Game Rule 96," Meredith said. "After a player serves his or her detention term, he or she will have his or her cell phone, GPS unit, and bank cards returned to him or her. He or she will be driven twenty-four miles in the direction of his or her choice."

"Sounds like you memorized the entire list of game rules," I said.

"I know them better than the multiplication tables," Meredith replied.

Right then, an orange guard entered the rec room with a cart loaded with breakfast food. While Meredith and I feasted on cheese omelets, I continued to ask questions.

"What do you know about the twenty-four teams in this Great Gloomy Game?"

Meredith tapped her lips with a napkin. "There's the Bly Voyage Project, the Cook Voyage Project, the Drake Voyage Project, the Fossett Voyage Project, the Gagarin Voyage Project, the Kunste Voyage Project, the Tereshkova Voyage Project, and others," she recited. "Each of them named after a famous circumnavigator. Did you know that Dave Kunste *walked* around the world? Valentina Tereshkova was the first woman to orbit the earth in space. Steven Fossett flew around the world solo in a balloon, and Nellie Bly was a newspaper reporter who circled the earth alone in 1889."

"How many other players do you know?"

"Not many. It's hard finding reliable info about players. Remember, it was an accident that I met you. But I do know many of the team producers."

"All members of the League of Royalty without Domains?" I asked.

Meredith nodded. "The BVP producer is Chief Montezuma XXX, who has no Aztec realm to rule.

The John Glenn Voyage Project's producer is Emperor Napoleon VIII, who lacks an empire. Sheik Kaput, of the Drake Voyage Project, ruled a sheikdom in the Arabian Desert until the map companies forgot to draw it on their maps. Eventually, so many people forgot about the territory that it ceased to exist. The CVP producer, Old King Cole, is a sad soul. One winter he lost his small Himalayan kingdom in a snowstorm. King Cole and his three fiddlers are still searching for it."

"And there's Baron von Sheepsbottom from TVP," I said. "He paid me a visit last night."

"The baron's ancestors once ruled half of Europe and Asia," Meredith explained. "They were greedy hunters. They hunted so much that every animal in their empire became extinct. Your producer and the TVP producer have bad blood between them."

"Gunter the Hunter," I remembered.

Meredith and I spent the morning watching videos, playing tennis, and swimming. But by noon we were bored. While we lolled by the pool in our bathing suits, I kept studying the sunflower field less than ten yards away.

"You know, Meredith," I said, "I've been thinking—is there a game rule that prevents a player from escaping a detention center?"

"No, but players would be foolish to try," she replied. "They'd be stuck in the middle of nowhere without a phone, GPS, or money to buy a ticket onward. Local police would soon find them and deport them straight home. Game over."

I cased out the sunflowers some more. "That's why this DC isn't hard to leave," I said. "Only two clunky guards and no fence."

Meredith looked at me with interest.

"Here's what we should do," I went on. "Get dressed, pack some food, and take off through the sunflower field. It's endless. We could make it all the way to the main road without being spotted."

"And why would you want me to escape with you?" Meredith asked. "We're opponents, foes, rivals. Remember?"

"Because two kids can travel cheaper and safer than one," I said. "Besides, two twelve-year-olds stand out less. You said you were in this game to win, Meredith. Well, the TVP player, Chukudifu, will beat us both if we don't try something daring. You with me or not?"

Meredith rose from her chair. "When do we leave?"

I looked at my watch. It said 1:50. "Plenty of daylight left. Why not now?"

After changing and stuffing our backpacks with blankets and sandwiches, we checked the hallway for guards.

"All clear," Meredith whispered.

"We're out of here," I said.

Together we shouldered our packs and ran from the rec room. We charged across the tennis court and dove into the sunflowers. Almost at once, dogs started barking inside the château.

I stopped, crouching low. "Those dogs sound fierce," I said. "Do we go or stay?"

Meredith answered by sprinting up a row of sunflowers. Without looking back, I followed.

I ran, thinking of only one thing. Ferocious canines! Dogs biting my ankle. Dogs leaping on me from behind. And the faster I ran, the louder the barking seemed to get. At one point, feeling dog breath on my heels, I sprinted past Meredith.

Finally, after many minutes, the barking stopped, and so did we.

Meredith bent over laughing. "Go, dog," she said.

"I'm too hot to hoot," I replied, breathing hard. "What's so funny? Those dogs almost ripped us apart."

"Game Rule 73 states that no animals can be used to chase or track players," Meredith said. "That barking was just a recording."

"Now you tell me," I muttered.

Tall sunflower stalks surrounded us. Only a thin strip of sky was visible above their nodding yellow heads.

"What's the plan, MVP man?" Meredith asked. "Soon every team tracker in France will be after us. They can collect two tracking fees in one shot. Meanwhile, it's a long walk to Paris. We don't even know which way to go."

I looked up. Every sunflower faced the same direction, westward. I had watched the big blossoms all morning follow the sun across the southern sky.

"Thataway," I said, pointing north.

We hiked through the sunflowers for maybe a half mile. Finally, ahead, daylight greeted us along with the rumble of an engine. We emerged into an area of flattened sunflower stalks. Nearby, a farmer drove a tractor, towing a cart loaded with yellow blossoms.

"Hey! Hello!" I shouted to the farmer. "We're lost! Can you help us?"

To my surprise, Meredith called to the farmer in French. He stopped his engine, and we ran up to him. Meredith and he talked back and forth while I stood there like a dummy.

"Come on," Meredith finally said. "This is Monsieur Canard and he's offered us a ride to his farmhouse. I told him we're backpacking around France for the summer. He thinks we're a lot older than twelve."

"*Merci! Merci!*" I called out, and we climbed onto the mountain of sunflowers in the cart.

At the farmhouse Madame Canard invited us to dinner. We ate outside at a table under a big tree. To convince Monsieur Canard that I was older, I sipped the red wine he poured me.

Of course, Meredith did most of the talking.

"Good news, Adam," she said. "Monsieur Canard will drive us to a nearby train station and buy us tickets to Paris."

"How will we pay him back?" I asked. "I hate handouts."

"He told us to pass the favor along to other needy travelers on our trip," said Meredith.

—

Soon we were riding in Monsieur Canard's truck along a narrow country road. We entered a village with a small rail station and caught a train to Paris. We arrived there shortly after sunset.

"So, MVP man, what now?" Meredith asked in the station lobby. "Do we wait here for a tracker to find us, or do we look for a park to sleep in tonight?"

I studied the large train departure board on the wall.

"I've got a better idea," I said. "MVP planned for me to be in Paris last night. Right? That means they reserved a train ticket for me for today. Who knows what city they scheduled for me to travel to next—Berlin, Amsterdam, Venice, or maybe Rome—but it must be east of here."

I found the ticket counter. To my relief, the woman there spoke English. Holding out my passport, I said, "My name's Adam Story. I'm supposed to meet my parents somewhere tomorrow, but I forgot what city. They reserved a ticket for me."

The woman gave me an I-don't-believe-a-word-of-it look, but she checked her computer anyway. "*Bon.* Here it is. Adam Story," she said. "A first-class sleeper to Copenhagen. I see you missed your train this morning, but your parents bought you another ticket for tonight."

"That's right, Denmark," I said. "I should have remembered."

Meanwhile, Meredith was studying a Paris map on

the wall. Was it time to ditch her? No, I couldn't do that.

"Did my parents get my message about bringing a friend along?" I asked the ticket woman.

"The reservation is for one person," she replied.

"Then could I exchange my first-class sleeper for two plain second-class tickets?"

The woman tapped more computer keys. "*Bon.* It's nearly the same price," she said. "But you must hurry. The train leaves from another station, Gare du Nord, in twenty minutes."

The woman handed me two second-class tickets to Copenhagen along with a few coins called euros for change.

Good thing Meredith had studied the Paris map. Using the euros to buy Metro tickets, we quickly found the correct subway to whisk us across town to the Gare du Nord. I was back at the station where I had first landed in Paris.

"Good show, Adam," Meredith said. "We make a good team."

We boarded the Copenhagen train as the conductor was blowing his whistle. Our second-class car had compartments that you entered through a sliding glass door. Each compartment had vinyl seats facing each other. But backpackers and their gear occupied most of them.

When we finally found two empty seats, we threw our bags on an overhead shelf and sat down. Our compartment mates were two twenty-something guys from

Iowa and two twenty-something girls from Canada.

"Paris was a party," one American announced to the Canadians. "We partied for two days."

"We're traveling all over Europe," the second man bragged. "After Copenhagen, we're going to Amsterdam to party some more."

Meredith and I exchanged smiles. How could we explain what we'd been through and where we were going?

With a jerk the train departed Paris. Our around-the-world trip had resumed. The next morning we'd be in Denmark.

KØBENHAVN

At last, the station sign appeared out the train window. Groggy and sore, I climbed down to the platform. Our compartment mates had chatted most of the night, so Meredith and I got little sleep.

"Cool Copenhagen!" one American cried.

"Paaarty!" called the other.

"Day 14," I grumbled. "Another day, another country."

As I had figured, another first-class train ticket was waiting for me at the station ticket counter, this one to Stockholm, Sweden. We exchanged it for two second-class tickets. With two hours before the train departed, Meredith and I went for a walk.

We strolled along a wide street lined with shops that were just opening. A bright yellow bus rolled by and deposited people beside the train station. Cinnamon rolls, frosted buns, and fresh bread crammed the shop windows. The smell made my stomach complain with loud growls and gurgles.

"I'm starved," I said. "How are we going to eat today?"

"Something will show up," Meredith replied. "It always does."

Typical Meredith. Never worried, never in doubt.

Another bus came down the street. It stopped twenty yards from us and a solitary man stepped off. He wore a black suit and a black turban. I gulped hard. The man was Prince Oh.

"Wait here," I said to Meredith, and ran up to my producer.

Marco Polo, the mongoose, jumped out of the prince's pocket as I approached. It sat on his left shoulder, glaring at me.

"Good morning! *Bonjour! Goddag,* Adam Story!" Prince Oh called out. "You've certainly come a long way since last we met. Your escape from the detention center was brilliant. When you collected the train tickets in Paris, I knew with certainty where to find you."

"Why didn't you tell me about the game?" I said. "Why did you deceive me?"

The prince's black eyes flashed. The mongoose  turned a circle on his shoulder. "I kept certain details about the GGG teams and rules because I knew you're not a team player and you certainly don't play by rules. You're an individual, Adam Story. You choose your own path. I was certain that if you'd known about the other players, you wouldn't have accepted the MVP challenge."

Although I didn't say so, the producer was right. That's the way I am.

"So what's next?" I asked.

"As you know, this is the single time during the game that we're permitted to meet. I've come to Copenhagen to warn you of certain dangers that lie ahead, Adam Story. If you wish, this certainly is the best time and place to end your journey and opt to go home."

"What's the MVP plan?"

"We've arranged for you to travel through Scandinavia by train and ferry and on to Moscow, Russia," Prince Oh said. "From there, you will take the Trans-Siberian Railway to the Pacific Ocean. Asia will certainly be the most remote and dangerous part of your journey. If you run into trouble in Siberia, Adam Story, it will take our pilots a certain amount of time to come to your aid."

"I know about the Trans-Siberian Railway," I said. "Sitting eight days on a train seems a breeze. What else?"

The mongoose turned another three-sixty on Prince Oh's shoulder.

"We've analyzed the darts that struck you," the prince went on. "One GGG team is certainly not playing fair. We found a potent sleeping dope on the dart tips. LORD officials learned that a certain producer has trained ninety-nine teenagers, seventeen and eighteen years old, from around the world to hunt down players. LORD named these teens 'stoppers.' Stoppers are appearing on every continent. They have an uncanny knack for finding players and giving them a twenty-four-hour nap. That's for certain."

"Tranquilizer darts don't worry me," I said.

"Fortunately, the northern route should be clear of many trackers and stoppers," said Prince Oh. "We believe there are seventeen players left in the GGG. Three are in detention centers. The rest are spread around the globe. As far as MVP knows, you are presently in fourth place. The leader, Chukudifu from TVP, is one and a half time zones ahead of you."

"And he's going in the opposite direction," I mentioned. "Anything else?"

"There's another issue we certainly need to discuss. That certain someone, that certain GVP player who's traveling with you. She must go her own way."

We both looked toward Meredith, who was sitting on a bench watching us.

"Meredith's helped me a lot," I said. "She knows the game well."

Prince Oh reached into his pocket and brought out a blue cell phone, a GPS unit, and two blue cards, an ATM card and a credit card. I took them and dropped them into my Reno tote bag.

"The GVP player is your opponent, Adam Story," he said. "The stakes in this game are certainly great, and she's untrustworthy. If she contacts her team, GVP trackers will certainly find you and destroy all your chances of winning."

"Meredith wouldn't double-cross me," I insisted.

"Adam Story, your train arrives in Stockholm at 2:50. Tonight you must be on the ferry to Finland, leaving at 6:00. You'll be in Helsinki early tomorrow. MVP has made all the reservations for you, first-class. But, Adam Story, before you board that ferry, be certain to part with the GVP player. You'll have until 5:00 p.m. At that time, as certain as homework, I will send a squad of MVP trackers to capture Meredith Emerson. Do you understand?"

I nodded. "Certainly."

Prince Oh handed me some Danish coins, called kroner. "Get yourself some breakfast before the train leaves."

As he spoke, a yellow bus squealed to a stop in front of us. The mongoose dove back into the prince's pocket, and Prince Oh walked to the open door. Before mounting the stairs, he turned and bowed his head.

"Good luck, Adam Story," he called out. "The MVP team is counting on you. My noble ancestors of Babababad thank you. That's for certain."

Loaded with pastries we bought from a shop, Meredith and I returned to the train station. We were delighted to find an empty compartment on the Stockholm train.

The train departed Copenhagen, but we saw little of Denmark through the windows. After a few kilometers, the train dipped into a long tunnel, and when it

emerged we were in Sweden. The scene outside turned to flowery fields and woods of white paper-birch trees.

As we ate sticky buns and rolls, Meredith asked, "So why are you doing this?"

"Doing what? The Great Globby Game? For the money, I guess. I also like adventure."

Meredith's face softened. "No, I mean, why are you helping me? I saw your producer hand you the phone, GPS, and bank cards. You could have easily left me back in Copenhagen."

I didn't know how to answer this. Meredith's company was good, and I didn't want anything to change. Still, I resisted telling her about Prince Oh's ultimatum. Five o'clock or else. What would I do in Stockholm?

Having had little sleep the night before, I stretched out on the vinyl seat and closed my eyes. I conked out in seconds. Meredith shook me awake in the Stockholm train station.

3:25 by the station clock.

I had made a decision. Meredith and I would drive straight to the Finnish ferry. We'd be on board before Prince Oh released the MVP trackers.

After withdrawing Swedish money, called kronor, from an ATM, I bought a Stockholm map.

"The ferry pier is a long walk from here," I told Meredith. "We better take a taxi."

"Nonsense, I want to see Stockholm," she insisted. "We haven't walked much. We need the exercise."

"OK. But let's walk fast."

As we left the station, Meredith sniffed the air. "Have you noticed that every city has a special smell?" she said. "LA smells like concrete. Paris smells like lavender, and Stockholm smells like a beach just after a storm."

"This city seems more water than land," I said. "According to the map, it's a maze of bridges."

We hiked over several bridges, passed the royal palace, and entered the old part of the city. Here the streets were hilly, cobbled, and narrow. From the top of one hill I spied the ferry pier in the distance. A line of cars was snaking into the back end of an enormous white shoebox of a ferry.

4:35, according to my watch.

"Let's go, Meredith," I said.

"What's your hurry?" she said. "You have a credit card. Let's do some shopping. How often will we be in Sweden?"

I had a credit card all right, I thought. With that and

the ATM card and all the other tracking chips in my pocket, the MVP trackers would have no trouble finding us the instant the clock struck 5:00.

Meredith turned onto a dark cobblestone lane that led uphill.

"Meredith, no!" I called out, running after her. "We haven't time. We must get to the ferry."

She was halfway up the hill when I spied them. Two men wearing yellow nylon jackets stood at the top.

4:47.

"You're early!" I nearly shouted. But I didn't. Instead, I ducked into a coffee shop. From there, I had a good view of the yellow men out the front window.

Meredith saw the trackers, too. She plastered herself against a storefront as the men started down the hill. I could see everything, and I held my breath. I saw the men stop by Meredith. I saw them exchange a few words with her and then continue down the hill. They ran past the café where I was hiding.

That's when it dawned on me. Those men weren't

MVP trackers trying to catch the GVP player, Meredith. They were GVP trackers trying to capture me.

I waited in the coffee shop hardly breathing. Had Meredith really turned me over to GVP trackers? Maybe it was just a coincidence that her team's trackers were in Stockholm. That was it. Chances were, MVP trackers had already captured Meredith. Either way, I had to reach the Finnish ferry as fast as I could.

I stepped out onto the cobblestone lane. Meredith and the men in the yellow jackets had vanished. With my blue pack bouncing on my back, I started to run. I left the old section of Stockholm and arrived at the ferry pier just as the ferry's car gate was closing.

After buying my ticket, I charged up the passenger ramp. Who knew how many trackers were on my tail? The inside of the ferry resembled a shopping mall more than a ship. Heading to my cabin, I passed candy stores, jewelry stores, clothing stores, and more stores. I entered my room and locked the door.

A jolt signaled the ferry's departure. Out the round cabin window, I watched Stockholm grow smaller as we slid out onto the Baltic Sea.

"So long, Meredith," I said, waving to the waves.

Hardly had I spoken when a rap came on the door. Not knowing the Swedish or Finnish words for "Come in," I opened the door myself. There stood Meredith, her blue hair dangling in her face, her blue backpack on the floor. Tears stained her cheeks.

"I'm—I'm so glad I found you, Adam," she sniveled. She wiped her nose with the sleeve of her blue sweatshirt. "I had to lie like crazy to get on board. Y-y-you must buy me a ferry ticket right away or they'll arrest me as a stowaway."

"You *are* a stowaway," I said.

Meredith's lips quivered. "What do you mean? We're still a team, aren't we?"

"That's what I thought until we met those GVP trackers back in Stockholm," I said.

"Adam, those men surprised me as much as they surprised you. And do you know what they told me on the hill? Five MVP trackers were in Stockholm searching solely for me. So guess what I thought? You had the phone and everything. But no, I said to myself. Adam Story would never turn me in. I'm here because we made an agreement to stick together."

Meredith sobbed and sniffed some more. She stood in the doorway with her raggedy blue hair, and I felt awful for all the bad thoughts I had had about her.

I picked up her backpack. "Come on in. I'll buy your ticket, and then we'll go have dinner, something called a smorgasbord."

A smorgasbord, we soon discovered, was a huge buffet with a dazzling variety of food. Here is a list of the smorgasbord food I piled on my plate:

1. Smoked salmon
2. Pickled herring

3. Reindeer meat
4. Swedish meatballs
5. Cheesy potatoes
6. Macaroni salad
7. Lots of little red crayfish
8. Black bread
9. Slabs of white cheese
10. Cloudberry pie

Meredith and I sat at a window table. The huge shoebox glided through a channel studded with rocky islands. Each island had a red cabin on it. A blue and yellow Swedish flag fluttered in front of each one. Blond women and children waved to us, and we waved back.

"Look how sunny it still is, although it's nearly ten p.m.," Meredith said.

"We're on the top of the world," I said. "Almost."

After dinner I found an ATM and withdrew money. Finland, like France, uses euros. Next, we walked to the bow of the boat, where backpackers had carpeted the deck with sleeping bags. We leaned over the railing. The ship cut a large U in the Blue-Violet water.

With Meredith beside me, I pulled out my new phone and called home. Mom answered in a groggy voice. "Adam, is everything all right? It's so early."

I had forgotten that it was morning in the other half of the world.

"I'm fine, Mom."

"So you're heading for your new camp today?" she asked.

New camp? Panic. What camp was I scheduled to be moving to this week?

"I hear it's very nice, Mom," I said. "Lots of water and everything. How's work?"

We talked for another ten minutes, and when the call ended, I held the phone over the railing.

"Phone overboard!" I shouted, and let go.

"What did you do that for?" Meredith cried.

Without answering, I took out the GPS unit and plastic cards and tossed them in the water as well.

"Are you crazy?" said Meredith. "Now we can't call for help. Now we can't get money."

"Now no team can track us," I said.

"Now we're really on our own," Meredith said.

"We're a new team, Meredith," I said. "We can call it the Phileas Fogg Voyage Project."

"The what?"

"PFVP, named after Phileas Fogg, who tried traveling around the world in eighty days in Jules Verne's book."

"Did he make it?"

"With only seconds to spare," I said. "But, of course, that book was fiction and written over a hundred years ago. We'll make it around in plenty of time."

Time Zone 11, EEST (East European Summer Time)

We both slept soundly that night, and early the next morning we disembarked in Helsinki, Finland. As we

walked down the gangway, Meredith took a deep whiff of the morning air.

"Helsinki smells like Christmas," she said. "Pine mixed with gingerbread."

On a hill above the city the cathedral's Green-Yellow dome glistened in the morning sun. Near the port a morning food market swarmed with Finns. We bought bread and berry jelly and sat on a bench to eat.

"Day 15," I announced, pulling a white poker chip from my pocket. "Eleventh time zone."

I inserted the chip beneath the bench seat.

The train station was a short walk from the harbor. When we arrived, it was still crowded with morning commuters. Many people wore yellow—yellow dresses, yellow jackets, yellow hats, yellow T-shirts.

"Yellow seems to be a popular Finnish color," said Meredith.

"Or else this station is crawling with trackers," I said.

Our plan was to find a train to Russia, first to St. Petersburg and then on to Moscow. We both had Russian visas in our passports. We searched for the international ticket counter, but the Finnish signs completely puzzled us. We couldn't tell which signs read "Tickets," "Departures," "Gift Shop," or "Waiting Room."

One sign, however, I recognized—a blue stick-figure of a man.

"The international symbol for a men's restroom," I said. "I'll be right back."

I left Meredith standing in the station lobby with our bags. I'd been in the men's room only ten seconds before a scream came from outside. I rushed back to the lobby to find a crowd surrounding a figure lying on the cement floor.

"Meredith," I muttered.

I elbowed through the mob and knelt by her side. She appeared to be asleep.

Across from me crouched an old man. The sleeves of his blue denim shirt were rolled up. Only a few wisps of gray hair remained on the top of his head.

"What happened?" I asked.

The man reached out and slipped a feathered dart into my palm.

"We must get your friend out of the station before the police arrive," he whispered in English.

"Who are you?" I asked.

"Later," the man said. "The dart came from the dark corner over there. You are still in danger. Now say something to these people."

I understood and looked up. "She'll be all right. She's my sister," I said. "She has fainting fits all the time. She just needs some fresh air."

The old man slid both arms under Meredith and lifted her. She dangled as if wilted, her blue hair swishing back and forth. The man's muscles bulged as he carried her toward the station entrance.

A Finnish police officer approached me. "Are you sure your sister is all right?" he asked.

I grabbed our backpacks. "Sure, she'll snap to in a few minutes. Thanks for your concern. What's 'Thank you' in Finnish?"

"*Kiitos*," the officer answered.

"*Kiitos*," I said to the people still standing there.

I charged after the old man. "Where are you taking her?" I asked. "You're not a tracker or a pilot. What team are you on?"

"My name's Shypoke Crisp," the man said. "I'm just an old sailor who's been noticing a lot of strange things around this station the past few weeks. Do you know what's on that dart?"

"Sleeping dope," I said. "She'll be knocked out for twenty-four hours."

"Then we'll go to my cabin," the man said. "My truck is parked nearby."

"No, we can't," I said.

"You'll have to trust me," Shypoke Crisp said. "I know about the game. I know you are trying to circle the world in forty days. And I know if this girl is found by the police, you'll both be sent home to your parents."

We rode in the back of a battered pickup truck. I sat on a bale of fishing net. Meredith, asleep, lay on a stack of burlap sacks, her head in my lap. Shypoke Crisp turned often in the driver's seat to check on us. He drove eastward along a four-lane highway. After two hours, according to my watch, he turned onto a narrow dirt road. With each bump I flew about a foot in the air.

Dark, smoky clouds had gathered in the southern sky. Thunder rumbled in the distance. Zigzags of lightning, rarely seen back home, lit the horizon.

"I must trust this fisherman," I told myself. "What other choice do I have? The PFVP team is in trouble."

The road ended on the shore of the tossing sea. On a rocky point beyond a stand of birch trees stood a log cottage. A narrow outhouse stood in back. Another log building—a sauna, I later learned—sat on the water's edge. At the end of a wooden dock an old fishing boat rocked side to side.

Shypoke Crisp leaped from the truck and lifted Meredith out of the back. Without a word he carried her down a path into the cottage.

Lugging our backpacks, I followed him. By the time I reached the doorway, Meredith lay on a bed with a quilt over her. Shypoke knelt before a stone fireplace, building a fire.

The cottage was small but welcoming. Colorful braided rugs covered the shiny wooden floor. The birch furniture—a rocking chair, two stools, and a table—appeared handmade. Items I'd seen in seafood restaurants crowded the walls: glass floats, seashells, colorful coral, a brass bell, and ropes tied into fancy fisherman knots.

"Take off your shoes," Shypoke called to me. "And don't expect electricity or indoor plumbing. Finns prefer their cabins simple."

I stepped into the room and sat on the end of the

Meredith's bed. Wind howled through the chinks in the cabin walls. Outside the window, the birch trees switched back and forth, and foamy waves pounded the rocky shore.

"Big storm approaching," Shypoke Crisp said. "We'll be warm and safe here."

"How do you know about the Great Global Game?" I asked.

"Old people have much time to sit and observe," he replied. "Last week I spied a Russian girl wandering around the train station. How odd, I thought, that a foreign girl so young would be traveling alone. When I questioned her—her name was Masha—she was eager to talk. She told me about the around-the-world race, about the teams, and about all the money involved. Masha was a player on the CVP team, the Cook Voyage Project."

"What happened to her?" I asked.

"Masha was nervous about taking the next leg of her journey into Europe. She missed her boat to Germany. A woman dressed in green arrived and put her on a train."

"A CVP pilot," I explained.

Shypoke poked the fire with a stick. "A few days later, a boy named Mark Setgo from Australia showed up. Same age. Twelve. Mark told me the same story about this GGG. He belonged to the Bly Voyage Project. He was about to take the ferry to Estonia when an American couple, both wearing yellow cowboy hats, led him out of the station."

"Trackers," I said. "Mark Setgo is either home by now or resting peacefully at the +2 Detention Center."

Shypoke Crisp rose and walked to the small kitchen. He returned with two metal plates of sausages and brown bread. We ate before the fire.

"So why are you helping us, Shypoke?" I asked.

He stared into the flames a moment before answering. "I admire what you young folks are doing," he said. "My life was once as full of adventure as yours. When I was still a teenager I joined the crew of a Finnish ice cutter that plied the frozen ocean north of Norway and Russia. Later, I was a member of several Arctic expeditions, one across Greenland and another to the North Pole. Afterwards, I built my fishing boat out there, *Moominpappa*, and fished the stormy seas off the coast of Iceland. How I long for those adventurous days of extremes and the unexpected!"

When we finished eating, the fisherman said, "Now it's time for a real Finnish tradition. I'll go fire up the sauna."

A half hour later I sat with Shypoke Crisp, buck naked, in the sauna by the sea. The cedar-walled room was so hot I could scarcely breathe. It got even hotter when Shypoke ladled water over the glowing rocks on top of the stove.

"Have you thought about your next move, Adam?" Shypoke asked while whacking his back with a leafy birch twig. "Where will you and Meredith go next?"

I shook my head. "It's too late to take the train to Russia. And I dread going back to that station."

"I believe I can help," Shypoke said. "I need to sail *Moominpappa* to the Russian coast tomorrow. I have business there. You and Meredith can be my crew. A Russian friend will drive you to Moscow."

"*Kiitos,*" I said. "It's like Meredith said—whenever things go bad on this journey, something happens to keep me going."

"Adventures are like that," said Shypoke Crisp. "The day can be gray and cold. Then the sun shines, and all is well again."

Suddenly the man let out a yelp and charged out of the sauna. Through the open door I saw him sprint down the dock and leap into the rough, frigid sea.

I settled for washing myself with a bucket of water. As I stood in front of the sauna putting on my pants, I watched Shypoke Crisp swim far from shore. The wind blew stiff and steady. The sky was like a chalky blackboard.

I turned to collect my towel from a peg on the sauna wall. That's when I saw it. Stuck in the door was a feathered dart.

"Who are those lads out there?" Shypoke Crisp asked.

"Stoppers," I said. "They're not supposed to be part of the game."

"They must be miserable out in the cold rain," Shypoke said.

"A producer has hired ninety-nine of them to delay game players by putting them to sleep," I said. "I can't guess how they got to this cabin."

Shypoke and I sat before a crackling fire inside the cottage. The door was locked. The white curtains were drawn across the windows.

"Better ease up on the blueberry juice," Shypoke said. "There'll be no trips to the outhouse tonight."

Shypoke Crisp had given me the hot beverage after I had summoned him from his swim. Blueberries grew all around the cottage. I had been guzzling the delicious drink.

Night had fallen, and the storm raged outside. I peered through a crack in the curtains. Whenever lightning flashed, I saw them, maybe twenty figures, standing among the birch trees. Each wore red sweatpants, red sneakers, and a red sweatshirt with the hood pulled up. Each sweatshirt had a large white number on the back. Stopper number 18 stood by Shypoke's truck, leaning on his long blowgun like a walking stick. Numbers 88 and 37 stood together by the outhouse. Number 11 stood on the dock by Shypoke's boat.

"The stoppers have surrounded the cottage," I said. "They're waiting for us to leave."

Shypoke Crisp held a finger to his lips.

Tap, tap, tap.

Footsteps sounded from the ceiling.

"They won't be able to enter my cottage," the fisherman whispered. "I built it for the Finnish winter. I come here when it's almost buried in snow. I must cut a hole in the ice for my sauna swim."

Meredith stirred on the bed. She whimpered and murmured goofy words.

"Nightmares," I said. "I was hoping one of us was having a peaceful night."

"Ever have misgivings about the girl?" Shypoke asked. "Few friendships are worth four million dollars. Somehow those hunters were able to follow us to this remote place."

For an answer, I stood and picked up Meredith's backpack, which lay by the door. I opened it and rifled through the contents. Near the bottom I found a blue cell phone and a GPS unit.

"She must have gotten these in Stockholm," I said. "So much for our PFVP team."

Day 15.

I must have dozed off for a few hours. I found myself sprawled in the rocking chair with a quilt over me. The smell of pancakes filled the cabin. Outside, waves slapped the shore and wind sang through the birch trees.

"Shypoke!" I called out, for he was nowhere in the room.

Meredith stirred on the bed. Her eyes opened.

"Madam, I'm Adam," I said.

"How long was I asleep?" she asked.

"A whole day. We're in a Finnish cottage by the sea. A stopper shot you. Now many stoppers have us surrounded."

"My head aches."

The cottage door swung open. Shypoke Crisp entered, followed by a blast of cold air.

"Perfect windy morning for dodging blow darts," he said. He wore a long black fisherman's slicker and hat. A feathered dart stuck out of his shoulder. Two more coats hung over his arm. He also carried a pistol.

"Only a signal flare gun," he said, noticing my alarm. "But the lads out there didn't know it. They kept their distance." He pulled the dart from his shoulder. "Fortunately, their darts can't pierce these rubber coats."

When Shypoke saw Meredith sitting up in bed, he nodded.

"*Hyvää huomenta*, Meredith," he said. "Hope you had a peaceful sleep. *Moominpappa* is ready to sail you to Russia. After breakfast we'll be under way."

A hot pancake breakfast sounded great. But what Shypoke Crisp brought from the kitchen made my stomach drop. The pancakes were dark red.

"Blood pancakes," he announced. "A special treat for

Finnish children. Pancakes dipped in reindeer blood and topped with cloudberry sauce. Help yourselves."

Reluctantly I poured the red syrup over a single pancake and tasted it. "Not bad," I said.

"We must thank Rudolph or whatever reindeer donated blood for our breakfast," said Meredith.

After we ate, Meredith and I put on the rubber coats. Their large size covered us from neck to foot. Sou'wester hats, the kind with long bills in the back, shielded our heads and necks.

Shypoke had floated the boat to a spot about halfway along the dock. Still, it was a good one-hundred-yard run from the cottage.

Out the window, nothing human moved. But the dart in Shypoke's shoulder was proof that the stoppers were still present. The wind blew in long gusts. This was ideal. No dart could fly straight.

Meredith and I grabbed our backpacks and stood at the door. Shypoke charged from the cottage first. Shouting things in Finnish, he waved his flare gun.

Meredith looked at me and I nodded. "One, two, three," we counted, and then we broke for the boat.

The long coat hindered my running. After a few steps I tripped and landed hard on my elbows. Meredith grabbed my arm and yanked me to my feet.

"Let's go, Popeye," she called out.

A feathered dart zinged past my head.

"I'm right with you!" I shouted.

We ran like crazy and didn't stop until we reached

 the sauna. Darts peppered the water as we raced up the dock and leaped into the fishing boat. Shypoke Crisp stood at the wheel with the motor revved.

The boat was a long stone's throw from shore before I looked back. The stoppers, all wearing red warm-ups, lined the shoreline. They stood as stiff as action figures, holding their blowguns by their sides.

"Welcome aboard *Moominpappa*," Shypoke shouted over the roar of the motor.

"First things first," I said. "My bladder is about to burst from all that blueberry juice." And I sprang to the stern to take a leak over the side.

Moominpappa had seen many years at sea. Her riggings were rusty and the deck bare of paint. Meredith and I sat on torn life preservers by the ship's hold. Instead of fish, stuffed burlap sacks filled the large open space.

Meredith nudged me. We both suspected the same thing. Shypoke Crisp was smuggling something into Russia. Drugs. What else could it be?

Since setting out to sea, the old fisherman had remained silent. He stood near the bow, eyes fixed forward, spinning the large spiked wheel one way and then the other as the boat pitched and tossed in the choppy water.

At the moment, neither the Finnish nor the Russian shoreline was in sight. Out there in the middle of the Gulf of Finland, the gale blew fierce. One after the other, waves taller than Shypoke raised and lowered *Moominpappa*. Good thing we were already wearing foul-weather gear or we would have been drenched.

"Adam, come here," Shypoke called out.

I rushed forward.

"You must take the wheel."

"What's wrong?" I shouted above the wind.

Shypoke rubbed his ankle and I knew the problem. A dart had struck him where his coat failed to cover.

"It only pricked the skin," he said. "But I don't know how long I can stay awake. The coast of Russia is a few hours away. We can't use lights or the radio—the Russian shore patrol would find us. Watch the compass. Keep *Moominpappa* headed at 120 degrees." He pointed to a lever near the wheel. "That's the throttle. Retain this speed as best you can. You must fight the wind or we'll be blown far off course and never reach the rendezvous point."

With these words Shypoke slumped to the floor.

Meredith rushed to my side. "Have you ever steered a boat before?" she asked.

I gripped the spokes on the wheel with both hands. "Only once, at Disneyland," I said. "A man let me drive the boat on the Jungle Cruise."

A huge wave slapped *Moominpappa*'s side. The bow pitched to the left, and I spun the wheel to the right.

The boat rocked violently and nearly tossed Meredith over the side.

"Easy does it, Popeye," she said. "This is the real ocean, not Adventureland."

For the next hour I steered *Moominpappa* while Meredith watched the compass. Waves battered the boat, and I swiveled the wheel until my arms ached.

"Land ho!" Meredith finally cried. She pointed to a brown smear dead ahead.

Minute by minute the Russian coast widened. We made out barren hills, birch trees, and beaches. The wind ceased, but in its place a thick curtain of fog descended over the sea. As the heavy gray mist swirled around us, the sun, sky, and coastline disappeared.

"Shypoke," I called out, shaking the fisherman. "Fog. I can't see. I don't know where I'm headed."

Shypoke Crisp, groggy and slack-eyed, struggled to his feet. He looked around and shook his head.

"Not good," he said. "We can't tell how far the wind and current have taken us off course." He held a pair of binoculars to his eyes, and again his head wagged.

"Would a GPS help?" I called out.

"Of course," Shypoke said. "But I have no such instrument. I make this trip by sight alone."

I stared at Meredith and she looked at the floorboards.

"But we have a GPS," I said. "A brand-new one."

Without a word Meredith retrieved the device from her backpack. She handed it to the fisherman.

Shypoke pushed some buttons and showed me the screen. "I've set the course you must take," he said. "The flashing X is our boat. This dot is our rendezvous, a cove due southeast of here. My friend Nina will be waiting there with her truck. She'll flash the headlights three times if it is safe to land."

"With the drugs," Meredith said under her breath as Shypoke closed his eyes and collapsed onto the burlap bags.

Meredith grabbed the binoculars and aimed them toward shore. I turned the wheel. The GPS buzzed, and I turned it some more. It buzzed again, and once more I corrected our course.

Thirty minutes later, a jagged coastline appeared through the fog. We heard waves crashing on the rocks.

Flash! Flash! Flash!

"That's her," Meredith cried. "I see a woman standing beside a large truck."

"Your GPS brought us here," I said. "I hope it didn't also bring stoppers and trackers."

Meredith gave me a look. "We're not there yet, Adam.

The truck is in a small inlet. You'll need more than your Jungle Cruise skills to get this boat in there."

I pulled the throttle, and the high whine of the engine deepened. The boat slowed to a near standstill.

"The wind's blowing us toward those boulders," Meredith shouted. "More speed!"

I nudged the throttle forward, giving the boat additional power. We glided slowly into the tiny bay.

Bruuuuup!

A rock struck the hull beneath my feet. It scraped along the bottom, bow to stern. A wave rolled under the boat and raised it. It swept us the rest of the way onto the cove.

I steered *Moominpappa* as close to shore as I thought safe and then cut the motor. On the pebbly beach, a woman wearing a leather jacket and high boots was pushing a rubber dinghy into the water.

"Good job, Popeye," said Meredith, throwing out the anchor.

The woman rowed the dinghy out to us. She climbed onto the boat and looked us over.

"I'm Nina," she said. "Shypoke Crisp radioed me this morning and mentioned his two passengers." She studied the fisherman. "But he didn't tell me he'd be taking a nap."

I explained about the dart.

"Well, if we're going to Moscow, you two must help me load the cargo into my truck," Nina said.

Both Meredith and I hesitated.

"We're not so sure about this," I said.

"What's in those bags?" asked Meredith.

Bending, the woman lifted a burlap sack from the hold. She smiled when she saw our concern.

"What do you think you smuggled into Russia?" she said. "You haven't known Shypoke Crisp very long, have you? He's a remarkable person."

Nina reached into the sack and pulled out a wool coat.

"Yes, we are smugglers," she admitted. "We smuggle second-hand clothes into Moscow for homeless children."

Time Zone 12, MSD (Moscow Summer Time)

We left Shypoke in the stern of *Moominpappa*, sleeping peacefully. Meredith and I wrote him thank-you notes. Nina placed a bottle of aspirin on his stomach.

The woman's truck was the kind used to deliver soft drinks, with roll-up side doors. A Coca-Cola bottle was painted on the rear, although odd, unreadable letters appeared on the bottle.

After loading the sacks of clothes, fifty in all, the three of us crammed into the front seat. We drove down a highway where I saw signs with more of the funny writing.

"We use the Cyrillic alphabet in Russia," Nina explained. "See that sign? It says 'Moscow 636 kilometers.'"

"Kilometers are another thing I find confusing,"

I said. "I wish the whole world would use the same alphabet and measurements."

Nina smiled. She was patient with my questions and comments.

"Since Russia became a capitalist economy about fifteen years ago, many people grew rich, but many remain poor," she said when I asked about the clothes. "Shypoke Crisp collects used winter coats, gloves, shoes, anything wearable from all over Europe. I deliver them to teenagers who live in train stations and sewers around Moscow. Now, will one of you tell me more about this Great Global Game?"

For the next twenty minutes Meredith entertained us by reciting game rules.

Here is a list of rules I remember:

Rule 27: No player's passport can be altered.
Rule 28: No bribe can be paid to a customs officer or ticket agent.
Rule 29: A player must travel by surface transportation only.
Rule 30: A player must be provided with quick and immediate transport home upon request.
Rule 31: No player can mention any aspect of the Great Global Game to a member of the press.

Some rules I already knew:

Rule 45: All players must wear something blue.
Rule 46: All trackers must wear something yellow.

Rule 47: All pilots must wear something green.

Rule 48: All producers must wear something black.

Rule 49: All players will be issued a GGG-approved blue backpack, blue cell phone, blue GPS unit, blue ATM card, and blue credit card prior to GGG starting time.

Rule 50: No player can leave home base before 8 p.m. GMT on July 14.

Other rules were new to me:

Rule 64: Any player who argues with a game referee's decision will be sent back one time zone.

Rule 65: Any player found breaking a local or country law will be sent back one time zone.

Rule 66: Any player found interfering with the progress of another player must not advance for twenty-four hours.

When the truck ran low on gas, we stopped to fill the tank and have dinner. Nina ordered. Hearing her switch from English to Russian was astonishing.

"I recognized the word *da*," I told Meredith. "That means yes."

"Duh," she replied.

The waiter brought three bowls of dark purple soup.

"Borsht," Nina explained. "Beet soup."

"Blood for breakfast and beets for dinner," I said.

"It looks like paint water after we've cleaned the brushes," Meredith mumbled.

Nina paid for the meal and helped me exchange my euros for Russian rubles.

"You'll need plenty of rubles if you plan to take the Trans-Siberian Railway," Nina said. "It's an eight-day train ride."

"Eight time zones," said Meredith.

"And lots of poker chips," I added.

That brought up the question of Meredith's blue ATM and credit cards and cell phone.

"Yes, I met Queen Mumumu in Stockholm, and she gave them to me," she explained. "I knew you had yours. It was only fair."

"But somehow stoppers can home in on the tracking devices implanted in those things," I said. "How else did they find us at Shypoke's cottage?"

"OK, in Moscow, I'll withdraw all the rubles I can from an ATM and buy our train tickets with the credit card," said Meredith. "Then I'll toss the cards, GPS, and phone, as you did. But let's agree to each make one last phone call."

"Deal," I said.

We arrived in the huge city of Moscow early the next morning. I rolled down the window and stuck out my head. A golden disk was peeking above the buildings.

"Good morning, sixteenth sunrise," I announced.

"Moscow smells like French fries," said Meredith.

At the street corner, two golden arches sat on a pole.

"Breakfast time," I said.

" I suppose you two deserve some familiar food," said Nina, and she turned into the McDonald's parking lot.

Except for the Cyrillic writing, the Russian McDonald's was no different from the ones in California, Nebraska, Paris, and Helsinki. The food pictured in the backlit signs above the counter was also the same. To order an Egg McMuffin, I pointed to the picture and said, "*Da.*"

After we ate, I buried a red poker chip at the base of the golden arches sign. Then I made my phone call to MVP.

Miss J answered. When I said my name, cheers erupted in the background.

"Adam, where are you?" Miss J asked. "MVP has been worried silly. We've been unable to track you for two days."

"I'm in Moscow," I reported, and that set off more cheers.

"Congratulations, Adam," Miss J said. "That places you in your twelfth time zone. Now listen, game referees have put out an alert. Customs officials stopped three players at country borders and sent them home. Someone had tipped them off. The GGG is still in full swing, but you must be cautious. Fortunately, you are already in Russia. Now, tell us your location, and an MVP pilot will come help you."

"I don't want MVP's help," I said. "I just called to tell everyone I'm OK." Then I disconnected.

Next, Meredith made her call to GVP. She said little more than "Uh-huh" and "Yes" and "I understand." When she was finished, she gave the phone and GPS to Nina as thank-you gifts.

Nina drove us to the station where trains left for Siberia. After helping us buy tickets, she said, "Now I must leave you. I have a truck to unload."

"Traveling means lots of sad good-byes," I said.

On our way to the train, Meredith cracked her two plastic cards into quarters. She held the pieces over a trash bin.

"So long, security," she said, and dropped the pieces one by one.

"The Phileas Fogg Voyage Project moves eastward," I said.

Time Zone 13, SAMST (Samara Summer Time)

The train's name was *Rossiya*, which meant Russian. Our first-class car had an aisle down one side and two-bedded compartments along the other. At one end of the car was a small room where the attendants, Anna and Otto, stayed.

Anna was round, short, and always happy. Her cheeks glowed red and her laugh was high and loud.

She spoke to us in one-word English sentences. "Hello. American? Sister?"

Otto was thin, tall, and quiet. He took charge of the silver tank, a samovar, which sat on a table outside his room. Water was always boiling inside the samovar, ready for any passenger who wanted tea.

"Otto sees Anna," Meredith said as the attendants led us to our compartment.

"He did, eh?" I replied, proud of my palindrome.

Soon after the train left Moscow, Meredith and I explored the rest of the train. Our car was "soft-class." The "hard-class" cars had side-by-side bunk beds. Mostly backpackers and Russian businessmen rode in hard-class.

A dining car served Russian food. We ate a cheap dinner of potato stew to save money.

That evening I lay on my bed studying a map of Russia while Meredith wrote palindromes in her notebook.

Da-dum, da-dum, da-dum, da-dum went the constant rhythm of the train wheels. *Da-dum, da-dum, da-dum, da-dum.*

"You know, Meredith, we've reached the halfway point," I said. "We're roughly 180 longitudinal degrees from California, and we've been traveling sixteen days. That's good progress."

"Bird rib. Dumb mud. Lion oil," she said. "Weird how 'Mom' and 'Dad' are both palindromes. Weird how I'm beginning to miss mine."

Da-dum, da-dum, da-dum, da-dum.

I looked up. A boy about our age stood in the doorway. He wore a blue jogging outfit. He said something in Russian and held up a chessboard.

"A GGG player?" I whispered to Meredith.

"If he is, he hasn't traveled very far," she replied. "He's Russian, and he wants to play chess."

I nodded. "*Da.*"

The boy sat on the edge of Meredith's bed. He set up a wooden chess set on the fold-down table between us.

"Yuri," the boy said, pointing to himself.

"Adam," I said. "That's Meredith."

Yuri checkmated me in ten moves and Meredith in twelve. He didn't seem to mind playing with rookies, and we played many games. I almost forgot there were stoppers and trackers in the world.

Da-dum, da-dum, da-dum, da-dum went the train.

Early the next morning, Day 17, the train stopped at a station. Meredith and I stepped outside. Russian women stood on the platform, hawking beets and potatoes.

I wedged a blue poker chip behind the train station sign and announced, "Thirteenth time zone."

Back on the train, we met the other "soft-class" passengers. Next door, two English women, Mrs. Whitherby and her granddaughter, Natty Whitherby, were also riding to Vladivostok. They rarely came out of their compartment except to complain to Anna and Otto. They were either too cold or too warm, too thirsty or too uncomfortable.

"The music on the speakers is too loud," Mrs. Whitherby griped.

"There's no ice in the restaurant," Natty Whitherby complained.

A New Zealand couple, Radar and Hannah, occupied the compartment on our other side. They had been traveling around the world for two years. They gave us lots of travel tips and told amazing stories about the countries they had visited.

"Do you ever get homesick?" Meredith asked them.

Radar cupped his hands to indicate the whole world. "*This* is our home."

"Once you catch the travel bug it's hard to stop," Hannah put in.

Neither Meredith nor I mentioned that we were trying to circle the world in six weeks.

Around noon, Radar, Hannah, Mrs. Whitherby, Natty Whitherby, and the other passengers in our car lined up at the windows.

"Come," said Otto, gesturing to Meredith and me.

Meredith and I joined them at the windows, although we didn't know why we were standing there. *Rossiya* was traveling through the Ural Mountains. The low hills covered with pine forests were beautiful, but they were the same hills and forests that had been out there all morning.

"Here, here," Anna called out.

Several passengers raised cameras.

Click! Click!

The train flew past a tall stone pillar.

Meredith and I shrugged at each other.

"Asia," Anna said, and then I understood. We had just passed the marker that separated Europe from Asia.

"Our last continent," I said to Meredith.

Part III
Asia

"Home is the place that makes you homesick."

Time Zone 14, YEKST (Yekaterinburg Summer Time)
Time Zone 15, OMSST (Omsk Summer Time)
Time Zone 16, KRAST (Krasnoyarsk Summer Time)

Da-dum, da-dum, da-dum, da-dum.

Each day the train rolled through a new time zone. Each morning I got off at a station and left a poker chip somewhere on the platform. I dropped a white one in a fountain. I planted a red one in a flowerpot. One station had a large bronze bust of a man's head, and I stuck a blue chip up his nose.

Da-dum, da-dum, da-dum, da-dum.

The days passed quickly, and I lost track of them. Radar lent me a calendar so that I could work out a schedule.

"Today's Thursday, August 1," I figured. "That means we arrive in Vladivostok on Monday, August 5. By Friday, August 23, I must reach the picnic table. That gives me eighteen days to cross the Pacific Ocean."

Da-dum, da-dum, da-dum, da-dum.

The scenery out the window became routine. Pine

tree after pine tree. Telephone pole after telephone pole.
Field after field of different crayon-box browns—Burnt
Sienna, Sepia, Mahogany, Chestnut.

Da-dum, da-dum, da-dum. Da-dum, da-dum, da-dum.

On board the train, however, I never got bored.
Someone always wanted to chat or play chess.

When I needed exercise, I walked down four cars to
Yuri's cabin. His parents, Neven and Eve, fed me black
bread, onions, and sausages. Once they opened a jar of
caviar. I put three of the tiny jelly-like sturgeon eggs on
my tongue and made a face.

Yuri's family laughed.

"Same result when I tried an American food called
peanut butter," Eve said.

Surprisingly, I saw little of Meredith. She had grown
quiet and moody. When I entered our compartment,
she left. When I stood in the hall, she lay on her bed.

One night, before turning off the light, I said to her,
"You know, Meredith, I've made more friends on this
train than during my entire fifth-grade year at school."

"Good for you," she said, in her leave-me-alone
voice.

"You know, Meredith, we could win this Great Goody-
Goody Game," I went on. "What's stopping us?"

"The Pacific Ocean," she grumbled.

"When we reach California, let's agree to arrive home
at exactly the same time," I said. "We'll split the prize
money even-steven."

"Okey-dokey."

"Do you know what I'll do with my money, Meredith? I'm going to buy a house for my mother and presents for everyone I met on this trip—Trav'lin' Man, Monsieur Canard, Shypoke Crisp, Nina, and all the train people."

"Go to sleep!"

Time Zone 17, IRKST (Irkutsk Summer Time)

Early the next morning the train stopped at a big city, Irkutsk. I'd always pictured Siberia as flat and barren, but here was a huge city with cars, tall buildings, trams, and crowds of people.

"Time Zone 17," I told Meredith, while rummaging through my backpack for a poker chip.

Without a word, she rolled over in bed.

On the platform I wedged a yellow chip behind the station clock. I was returning to our train car when a police officer in a gray uniform approached me. Vandalism? Littering? Would I be sent to a Siberian prison for leaving a poker chip?

Instead, the policeman asked in rough English, "Where you go?"

"Train. Vladivostok."

"With family?"

"*Da*. Mother and father. Train."

"Passport?"

"Train," I repeated, pointing.

The policeman held up a sheet of paper. "You see?"

I gulped hard. At the top of the paper was the word

MISSING. Below were pictures of Meredith and three boys our age.

Shaking my head, I hurried back onto the train. Meredith was asleep, but I rocked her awake.

"The police just showed me a picture of you," I said. "Like one of those missing-kid pictures on milk cartons. What does it mean? When did the police start searching for you? The Great Gloomy Game gets more dangerous every day."

"Go away," Meredith grumbled.

All afternoon the train followed the shores of a huge lake.

"Lake Baikal," Radar told me at the window. "Deepest lake in the world. A fifth of the world's fresh water."

"I once made a list of everything I wanted to see in the world," I said. "If I had known about Lake Baikal, I would have added it."

While we talked, Otto strolled down the aisle. "Party tonight," he announced. "Yuri's birthday. In dining room. Big party."

The party was great. Everyone came, even Mrs. Whitherby and Natty Whitherby. The train's cook baked a cake. Someone had blown up balloons. When Yuri entered the room, we shouted "Happy birthday!" in about ten different languages.

Anna wore a colorful Russian costume with lots of lace and ribbons.

Otto brought a triangular guitar-like instrument called a balalaika.

"Now music!" he announced.

While Otto played, Neven did a Russian dance. Hands on hips, he squatted low and kicked his legs out in time with the music.

The rest of us circled him and clapped our hands, shouting, "Hey! Hey! Hey!".

Radar and I entered the circle and tried dancing that way. I kept falling on my back, and everyone laughed. The music went faster, we danced faster, and the people clapped faster.

"Hey! Hey! Hey!"

I'll never forget how happy I was at that moment, with all my friends on *Rossiya*, the Russian train, in the middle of Siberia.

The party was still going strong when the train stopped at a small station. Some passengers disembarked here to catch another train past Mongolia to Beijing, China.

I glanced out the window and spotted Meredith standing on the platform. I thought she was getting fresh air, until I noticed her blue backpack. She never turned around. She just walked into the station.

My throat tightened. "So that's why Meredith's been moody lately," I told myself. "She must have been planning this all along."

After Meredith left, a tall man stepped onto the platform. He wore a yellow khaki shirt and pants. On his head was a yellow safari hat with the brim snapped up on one side and a leather strap under his chin.

Radar, who had drunk lots of vodka at the party, joined me at the window.

"Dig that dude's outfit," he said.

"He's a tracker," I told him. "And he's boarding the train."

Time Zone 18, YAKST (Yakutsk Summer Time)

I returned to my compartment and locked the door. Meredith's bed was made, and all traces of her were gone. I felt a mixture of emotions—betrayed and foolish, sad, and suddenly lonely.

"The Phileas Fogg team has officially disbanded," I said.

Most likely, Meredith had caught the train to China. Did she think that was a quicker way to California? Maybe it was. She'd be in Beijing tomorrow while I was still on this train with a tracker on board.

A knock on the door made me jolt.

"Adam, it's me, Radar."

I turned the latch and Radar entered quickly.

"The guy in the Jungle Jim getup came through the dining car, asking about you," he said.

"He's more like a bounty hunter," I said. "I need to tell you a story."

Radar sat on Meredith's bed while I filled him in on the details of the Great Global Game. Players, pilots, trackers, stoppers, producers, detention centers—there was a lot to tell.

"So you see, I'm trapped here," I said. "Trackers can be tricky. I'm not leaving this room until we reach the end of the line."

Radar rubbed his scraggly beard. "You lie low. Hannah and I will bring you food and guard your door."

I slept little that night. Too many thoughts about trackers and Meredith.

Early the next morning Hannah called from the hallway, "Up and at 'em, Adam! Breakfast!"

I unlocked the door, and she brought in a boiled egg, black bread, and tea.

"So how's our fugitive today?" she asked.

"I feel like a little kid who's being punished," I answered. I handed her a blue poker chip. "Would you leave this at the next stop? It's a memento of the eighteenth time zone."

Da-dum, da-dum, da-dum, da-dum.

Not much else happened that day, August 4. I remained in bed and read comics.

Da-dum, da-dum, da-dum, da-dum.

That evening someone knocked on my door.

"Who's there?" I called out.

No one answered.

"Radar? Hannah? That you?"

Still nothing.

Outside, I heard Mrs. Whitherby griping to Otto about a funny smell in her room, so I figured it was safe to check the hall. I cracked the door open. On the floor stood a liter-size bottle of ice-cold Mountain Dew.

 I looked up and down the hall but saw only the Englishwoman and the attendant. Radar and Hannah must have left the pop. They had brought me treats all day.

"Thank you, thank you," I said, bringing the jug into my compartment and relocking the door.

With no ice or refrigeration on the train, nothing cold had touched my throat since Moscow. I sat on my bed and raised the green plastic bottle to my lips. I guzzled half the contents before stopping.

"Thank you," I repeated, and drank the rest.

I slept fitfully again that night. A recurring dream featured me floating upon Lake Baikal. I awoke sometime during the night with an emergency. I had to use the WC at the end of the car. I turned on the light and checked my watch.

3:00 a.m.

Things couldn't wait. I had to go.

Da-dum, da-dum, da-dum, da-dum.

Slowly I opened the door. A single red bulb lit the corridor. Barefoot, I tiptoed out of my room. Mrs. Whitherby's snoring came loud and clear from her compartment.

Da-dum, da-dum, da-dum, da-dum.

I reached the toilet cubicle and did my business. When I returned to the room, much relieved, I noticed to my surprise that the light had gone out. As I fumbled for the switch, something dropped over my head. A heavy canvas bag. It ran down my shoulders, arms, hips, legs, and feet. A rough shove toppled me to the floor. I lay there unable to move.

Da-dum, da-dum, da-dum, da-dum.

"Bad boo-boo, Blue. Nothing makes you go like Mountain Dew," said a voice with a Texan accent. "Your seventy-two-hour detention has just begun."

Da-dum, da-dum, da-dum, da-dum.

Time Zone 18, JST (Japan Standard Time)

The next eight hours were the scariest, scruffiest, and smelliest of my journey. The inside of the canvas bag was inky black and reeked of dirty laundry. Only my sense of hearing told me what was happening.

Pa-bum, pa-bum, pa-bum went my racing heart.

Da-dum, da-dum, da-dum went the train.

After a long time the track noise stopped. We had arrived at a station.

"Alley-oop!" said the Texan voice, which no doubt belonged to the tracker on board.

The man lifted me by the waist and bumped me about like a sack of cement. A car door opened, and an engine started.

"Sorry, Blue, can't let you out of the bag yet."

I heard traffic. The car stopped and the door opened again. Now came seagull cries and waves lapping against wood.

"Upsy-daisy," the tracker said, and I returned to being a cement sack.

Footsteps on wood, keys rattling, a door opening, the putt-putt of a diesel engine, more seagulls, a distance foghorn, and more seagulls.

"The Pacific Ocean," I noted. "But where could this Texan tracker be taking me?"

Not for another two hours did I see daylight.

"OK, Blue, you can come out of your cocoon now."

After squirming from the bag, I found myself lying on the deck of a large yacht. My blue backpack and Reno tote bag sat beside me. The tracker in the yellow safari outfit stood at the helm.

He turned and doffed his yellow hat. "Dough Douglas is the name, Blue," he said. "Pleased to finally meet you. I've hunted big game in Africa for twenty years—lions, leopards, and the like—but no prey was harder to bag than you, Blue, a twelve-year-old boy. No wonder you're now the odds-on favorite to win the Great Global Game."

I stood up and rubbed my neck. "I thought GGG rules said no rough stuff."

"Apologies, Blue," the man said. "But to become a topnotch GGG tracker, I've learned how to avoid the zebra men."

"You mean game referees?"

"It's like big-game hunting in Africa," said the tracker. "The hardest part of going after rare rhinos and endangered elephants is dodging the game wardens."

Out the window I saw only ocean. "So what are you going to do with me, Dough? Mount my head on the wall?"

"The +9 Detention Center is outside Tokyo, Japan," the tracker replied. "We'll arrive early tomorrow. The guards at the DC are eager to meet you, Blue. You're quite a legend around this time zone. You and the GVP gal are the only players who have been bold enough to escape from a DC the entire game."

I relaxed on a deck chair. "I don't think I'll be trying any more escapes. A seventy-two-hour timeout sounds fine right now. Maybe I'll even go home."

"Either way, I get my bounty money," Dough said. "The GGG favorite is worth big bucks in the ex-royals' betting pool. Not only that, but my producer offered a whopping bonus to any tracker who could snag the MVP player. Odd bloke, that Gunter von Sheepsbottom. Always game to go big-game hunting. I've taken him on many a safari."

"Dough, do you know how many players are left in this Great Groovy Game?" I asked.

"Seven including you, Blue. Like big game in Africa, you blues are getting harder to find. After dropping you off, I'll return to the States to track the SVP player, Susie from the Seychelles. Susie from the Seychelles wished to go to the Washington seashore, so she boarded a bus marked 'Washington.' A thousand miles later she discovered her mistake: the bus was headed toward Washington, D.C. Bad boo-boo. Now Susie's stuck in the middle of Kansas. Look to starboard, Blue, that's Japan now."

Out the window a pink ribbon of land highlighted the horizon. From my birthday atlas I knew that Japan was surprisingly close to Russia. As I studied the distant shore, a jumbo container ship blocked my view. The yacht rocked in its wake.

"Lots of sea traffic today, Blue," Dough said. "Typhoon Tutti-Frutti is blowing south of here. Could be fortunate for you. Three GGG players are stuck in China, unable to cross the Pacific."

I slept for the rest of the day and through the night. Near sunrise I awoke. Land had appeared on both sides of us.

"Ohio, Blue," called Dough Douglas, still at the wheel.

"California," I replied.

"*Ohio*, you should know, means 'Good morning' in

Japanese," the tracker explained. "And we'll be docking in Japan shortly. We're in Tokyo Bay."

After winding through a labyrinth of sailboats, cargo boats, navy boats, and fishing boats, Dough moored the yacht in a large marina. I followed him to a yellow Jeep parked nearby. Soon we were driving through wooded hills above the sprawling city of Tokyo. A red rising sun, not unlike the red circle on the Japanese flag, rose above the city.

"You'll like this DC, Blue," Dough said. "You're lucky I didn't bag you farther down the line in the +10 time zone. That detention center is in northern Siberia."

The Jeep arrived at a small wooden house with a slanted wooden roof and walls made of paper. Two bearded guards dressed in orange jumpsuits stood on the front porch.

"Dough Douglas here, boys," Dough called out. "I'm delivering the MVP player. The very one. He's a bit pale and rundown, bruised slightly on the knees, but that's how I found him."

The guards stepped up to the yellow Jeep and bowed.

"Like I was saying, Blue," the tracker said to me, "you're a hero among these DC guards."

After Dough drove off, I followed the orange men into the Japanese house. They led me to a room with paper walls and straw mats covering the floor. In the center of the room was a futon, an inviting mattress-type bed.

"This will do," I said, and fell face first onto the futon.

August 6 and 7 passed uneventfully. I watched videos and played video games, ones that weren't released yet in the States. When I got bored, I strolled in the garden and fed the goldfish in the pond. During meals I practiced using chopsticks.

On the last evening of my detention I decided to do my laundry. When I dumped the contents of my backpack onto the futon, I found a note from Meredith.

Adam,

You probably think I'm a scumball for leaving you in Russia. Maybe you're right. But remember, this is a game, and I did what I thought I needed to do to win.

Here's a warning. When I called Queen Mumumu in Moscow I learned that fifty stoppers were waiting in Vladivostok. She didn't know why, but they were waiting solely for the MVP player. That's the main reason why I left the train. When I saw the tracker at the station, I knew you would be safe in a detention center.

Travel well,

Madam

The following morning, August 8, a white unmarked

van drove up to the house. My detention time was up. Game Rule 96 stated that after seventy-two hours players would collect their phones, GPS units, and credit cards and be driven twenty-four miles in any direction they chose. But I had no items to get back and no place I wanted to go.

I sat in the front of the van.

"*Ohio*," I said to the driver. "Drive anywhere you want."

A crow cawed from a nearby tree.

"You know, bird," I called out, "I'm the only person in the world who knows where I am right now, and even *I* don't know where I am."

The GGG driver had dropped me off precisely twenty-four miles from the +9 Detention Center. Wearing my bags on my shoulders, I sat on a guardrail surrounded by pine trees. The road signs with Japanese characters were useless, but I recognized a mountain, Mount Fuji, that rose to the south like a gray traffic cone.

"One more check for my wish-to-visit list," I told myself.

A car approached. Hoping that the signal for wanting a ride was the same in Japan as in America, I held out my thumb. The car stopped, and a Japanese woman rolled down her window.

"*Ohio*," I said.

"You need ride to Tokyo?" she said in broken English.

I leaped to my feet. "Yes, yes. *Ohio!*"

A second woman occupied the passenger seat, so I got in back. Ono and Ana were studying English at a university and wanted to practice.

"We want to speak English perfect," said Ono, the driver.

I noted the make of the car. "A Toyota," I said. "That's English forward and backward."

"What are you doing in Japan?" Ana asked.

"I'm playing a big game," I said. "I'm trying to beat other twelve-year-olds around the world."

The women looked alarmed.

Ono pounded the dashboard with her fist. "Beat?" she asked.

"No, no, not *that* beat," I said.

"Beat?" said Ana, flapping her arms.

I shook my head.

"Do you mean beat?" Ono said, pretending to play the drums.

I continued shaking my head. "Beat like in winning. I think I can still win the game. I just need to cross the Pacific Ocean."

"How you do that?" Ana asked.

"Beats me," I said, with a shrug.

Soon we reached the outskirts of Tokyo. Modern buildings glistened with glass, and everywhere neon signs flash-flash-flashed.

Ono drove me to the Tokyo Youth Hostel, a modern three-story building. The man at the registration desk exchanged my Russian rubles for Japanese yen and assigned me a bunk in the dormitory.

"It's a long way from The Plaza," I told myself. "But it's safe, clean, and cheap."

I found my bunk, a top one, and threw my backpack and tote bag up there. Below, an American backpacker was reading the *Lonely Planet Japan* guidebook. He wore cargo shorts and a ragged red T-shirt.

"I'm Adam," I said.

"I'm sure," he replied, without looking away from his book.

"No, that's my name," I said. "Adam Story."

The guy swung his legs off the bed and looked up at me. "And that's *my* name," he said. "Sure, Sure Thing."

"You're Sure?"

"Sure, I'm Sure."

Sure Thing was from San Francisco, and had flown to Tokyo that morning.

"I'm traveling around Asia on the cheap," he said. "I'll live on a shoestring until my money runs out."

"I'm on a budget too," I said, using my mother's expression. "I have only enough yen left for a few meals."

"So let's go hit the city, my man," Sure Thing said. "I'll show you how to get by for practically nothing."

We left the hostel and hiked to the nearest subway station. I approached the ticket vending machine that was covered with bewildering Japanese writing. Sure Thing, however, walked straight to the entrance turnstile. Before I knew what he was doing, he leapfrogged over the metal barrier.

"Come on," he called to me. "Free and easy-peasy. No one's looking."

As I stood trying to figure out the vending machine buttons, a Japanese man offered to help. I handed him two hundred-yen coins and soon had my ticket.

"Should have saved your money, my man," Sure said as we zoomed along in the super-modern subway car.

We got off in a busy area of Tokyo. The streets were packed with people and ablaze with lights. A line of vending machines stood outside each store. They sold everything from hot noodles to cameras, cans of beer, video games, socks, DVDs, comic books, and umbrellas.

"The Japanese must trust people," I said. "These machines wouldn't last one night on the streets of San Francisco."

"And these machines are an easy way to a free meal," Sure Thing said.

He pulled a small metal disk from his pocket. He inserted it into a vending machine that served pizza slices. To my surprise, a hot triangle of pizza slid out the slot at the bottom.

"These slugs work in machines all over Asia," Sure said. "Free and easy-peasy. I brought bags of them."

He handed me one of the blank coins. "Here you go."

"No, thanks," I said. "I still have a few yen left."

"What difference does it make?" Sure said. "Who's looking?"

I'm not sure why I took the slug. I wasn't even that hungry. But it was a huge mistake—a big boo-boo, as Dough Douglas would say.

The instant I plugged the slug into the vending machine, a loud whistle blew behind me.

I spun around. A gray-bearded man wearing a striped kaffiyeh, a GGG referee, stood there. Pointing a finger at me, he announced, "Adam Story, MVP player. A one-time-zone penalty for breaking Game Rule 65."

"What's going on?" Sure Thing asked. "Who's that guy? Is this some sort of game?"

"Yes, it's a game, all right," I said. "It's the Great Goosy Game, and I just got cooked."

An hour later I sat in a small black jet, flying westward above the clouds. The logo stenciled on the seatback in front of me showed Earth with "GGG" emblazoned across it. Inserted in the seat pocket was a newspaper called *GGG Daily News* #26.

The headline read:

MVP PLAYER VIOLATES GAME RULE 65!
Sent Back One Time Zone

Three Great Global Game referees occupied the front seats of the jet. Behind me sat four GGG producers dressed in black, and in the rear were two yellow trackers and three green pilots.

The producers introduced themselves as Queen Mumumu, of the Gagarin Voyage Project; Sheik Kaput, of the Drake Voyage Project; Czar Nicholas X, of the Kunst Voyage Project; and Maharajah Mah, of the Slocum Voyage Project.

Maharajah Mah leaned toward me. "Why in the world are you here, Adam?" he asked. Not much older than twenty, he wore black jeans, a black polo shirt, a black baseball cap, and black sunglasses. "Here you traveled three-quarters of the way around the world. Here you reached your eighteenth time zone with little help from your team. Here you escaped a DC, dodged stoppers, and endured ditsy Dough Douglas for a day. And then I hear you totally blew it in Tokyo. What in the world were you thinking? How in the world could you be so stupid?"

"Hear, hear!" called a pilot behind him.

"Ho, ho! That will surely cost you the GGG lead, son," said Czar Nicholas X, a round-bellied man with round red cheeks, a round red nose, and a snowy white beard. He wore a black hooded robe trimmed with ermine. "I had a bundle of money riding on you. Game Rule 65! Very naughty. We're lucky a game umpire caught you tampering with the vending machine before the Tokyo police did."

From the moment the referee had blown his whistle, I knew how foolish I'd been to hang around with Sure Thing. I remembered Game Rule 65 from Meredith: *Any player found breaking a local or country law will be sent back one time zone.*

The referee drove me on a motorcycle to the hostel to collect my gear. Afterwards, we drove to the airport, where the black jet was waiting.

At that moment a voice spoke on the loudspeaker.

"*Attention. This is a GGG special bulletin. The Bly Voyage Project player has just been released from the –8 Detention Center. Thank you.*"

"Right on, Mark Setgo!" cheered a tracker in the back of the jet.

I turned toward Queen Mumumu. "How's Meredith?" I asked.

The Polynesian producer leaned forward. Her wide hips spread the chair's armrests farther apart. She wore a loose black dress with a string of black pearls around her stout neck.

"My player's current longitude, latitude, and altitude are top secret," she answered. "But I can tell you, Miss Emerson is safe and in top shape."

Sheik Kaput held out a well-manicured hand. His skin was chalk white, a sharp contrast to the long black gown that he wore. A black handlebar mustache stretched across his doughy face.

"Bloody shame about Rule 65, my boy," he said. "I believe you met my bloody player, Pickles Goodhaven, before he bowed out of this bloody game."

"Pickles was at the +1 Detention Center with me," I said.

"Bloody boy managed only two bloody time zones," said the sheik. "No bloody backbone."

"So where are the refs taking me?" I asked the producers.

"Ho, ho! Hong Kong, most likely, son," Czar Nicholas X said.

"And who owns this jet?"

"We're on a GGG shuttle," Queen Mumumu explained. "A fleet of these jets transport referees to observation spots around the globe. Producers also use them to check on their teams. Now, with the game winding down, out-of-service trackers and pilots are on board, returning home."

"Two bloody weeks left, and some bloody producers already have bloody players on their bloody home stretch," Sheik Kaput grumbled. "Bloody shameful that an MVP pilot wasn't there to warn you about bloody Rule 65, my boy. It's bloody hard to imagine how Prince Oh could have made such a bloody slip-up."

"I hear it's more foul play," Maharajah Mah called out. "The GGG has been plagued with irregularities. The league must hold a hearing. Where in the world did those stoppers come from?"

At the mention of stoppers, the three referees in front flinched.

"Ho, ho! There hasn't been a LORD scandal like this since my ancestors lost their claim to the land around the North Pole," said Czar Nicholas X. "Ho, ho, hooey!"

"That was because there's no bloody land at the bloody North Pole," said Sheik Kaput. "Only bloody ice. Bloody dolt."

"Attention. This is a GGG special bulletin," the intercom voice repeated. *"The Fossett Voyage Project player has just been eliminated from the GGG for accepting a ride in a helicopter. Thank you."*

More cheers came from the pilots in back.

"Ho, ho, ho-hum!" called the czar. "I had a whole lot of money bet on that player as well."

"There's something about the whole Great Gooey Game I don't understand," I said. "Why do you producers care who wins? These jets, referees, trackers, pilots, and detention centers must cost zillions of dollars. What do you get out of this?"

Queen Mumumu shared looks with the other producers. Lowering her voice, she said, "It's not what the producers win that matters, Adam. It's what we must forfeit if our teams lose the game."

"When LORD members drew up the bloody rules for

this bloody game, they made the bloody stakes bloody high," said Sheik Kaput.

"Like what?" I asked. "You seem to have all the money you need."

"Ho, ho! Something nicer than money, son," said Czar Nicholas X. "Something we royals cherish above everything else."

"When my player, Susie from the Seychelles, quit the game, I knew what in the world it meant," said Maharajah Mah. "Here Susie's home now selling seashells by the Seychelles seashore, and I'm sitting here a ruined man."

"Hear, hear!" called a pilot in back.

At this point, a game referee, the one who busted me in Tokyo, turned in his seat. In a low, grave voice, he said, "Game Rule 101 states that each losing producer—every duke, duchess, marquis, earl, empress, viscount, count, countess, caliph, chief, sultan, pasha, shah, and rajah—must surrender his or her noble title."

I looked toward Sheik Kaput. "So since Pickles quit, you won't be a sheik anymore?"

"Bloody right. In two bloody weeks people will be calling me...it's too bloody embarrassing even to utter... *Mr.* Kaput. Bloody insufferable."

"And if Meredith loses, I'll be simply Miss Mumumu," said the GVP producer.

"And if Chukudifu loses, Baron von Sheepsbottom will be Mr. von Sheepsbottom," I said. "And Prince Oh will be Mr. Oh if I lose."

All four producers nodded.

"What if no player wins? What if no player makes it around the world in forty days?"

"The deal's off and no producer gives up a title," said the referee. "For this reason the final stages of the game will be extremely difficult for the remaining players. Hundreds of trackers will be after them."

I managed to sleep for a few hours before the jet started to descend. The sun was rising over Hong Kong. Out the window appeared a tall, modern city built on both sides of a bay. The layout was not unlike San Francisco's.

"We'll be landing shortly," a referee announced. "The MVP player must disembark here for his one-time-zone penalty. Don't forget to set your watch back one hour."

"Bloody about time," said Sheik Kaput.

Time Zone 17, HKT (Hong Kong Time)

6:13 a.m.

Tired and cranky, I stood alone in the Hong Kong airport. For the first time all journey, I hoped that an MVP pilot would greet me. But the only person in the terminal wearing green was a Chinese soldier.

"Where are pilots when you want them?" I grumbled.

I found the Tourist Information counter and collected a map of Hong Kong. At the airport bank I exchanged my remaining Japanese yen for Hong Kong dollars.

"A map and local currency," Radar told me on the Russian train. "Those are the first things to collect when you arrive in a new country."

Hoping for more shuteye, I walked to the waiting area. I had just claimed two soft chairs, one for my bags and one for me, when an announcement blared over the loudspeakers.

"Air France flight 202 now arriving from Paris at Gate 24."

I looked toward Gate 24. People streamed from the accordion tunnel that connected the airplane to the airport terminal. Among the crowd, whom should I spy but Dot and Tod, the twin trackers from France.

"How tempting," I told myself. "Why not give myself up right here? Right now." I patted my jeans pockets, still bulging with poker chips. "No, I'd hate myself if I did."

Before the twins could spot me, I grabbed my gear and shot out of the airport. From a quick look at my Hong Kong map I knew that a commuter train took people to the central section of the city. When I arrived, Queen's Road was just coming to life. Hong Kong was tall like New York, compact like London, bright like Paris, and busy like Tokyo. I found all the usual signs—KFC, Starbucks, Pizza Hut, and the Gap—except they were in Chinese as well as English. I entered a McDonald's and bought a cheap breakfast. "Never scrimp on food when you travel," Radar had warned me. "You'll need the energy."

While I ate my Egg McMuffin, I studied the Hong

Kong map. My plan was to walk to the cargo pier and find a ship that would take me to San Francisco. Radar had said that freighter captains sometimes offer passage to travelers in exchange for work.

The walk was long but enjoyable. I passed through a section of Hong Kong where small shops sold fruit and vegetables I'd never seen before. One store sold snakes, snake wine, and snake meat.

I reached Victoria Park. The large space had plenty of bushes and benches. Clearly I could spend the night there if I had to. Sleeping rough—that was what Radar had called it.

"Always be on the lookout for your next bed and meal," he had told me. "Often we were forced to sleep rough."

While cutting through the park, I passed a large statue of Buddha sitting cross-legged. I reached into my pocket and placed a white poker chip on Buddha's lap, where it sat among the flowers and beads other people had left.

"Don't know the time zone or even the date," I said. "That poker chip is for good luck."

The cargo pier was a puzzle of activity. I walked along the cement dock, marveling at the huge ships. They flew flags from countries all over the world.

I approached a Chinese man who looked as if he were in charge of a large freighter.

"Do you need a cabin boy or something?" I asked.

The man shook his head. "Stay home until you're

sixteen, kid," he replied. "After that you can think about running off to sea."

Some sailors gave me the same answer, and others only laughed. Finally I walked to the section of the harbor where tall cranes were loading large boxes onto container ships. The cranes reminded me of the giant Trojan horse we read about in Greek mythology. One by one, they stacked the multicolored containers on the flat ship decks like so many blocks on a kindergarten rug.

While standing by a crane, I overheard two men talking in English.

"Typhoon Tutti-Frutti's headed northward," one said. "You'll be able to leave tomorrow for Seattle."

"Aye, finally I can use my sea legs again," said the other. "My land legs don't work so well."

I approached the men. "Seattle?" I said. "I gotta get to the West Coast fast."

"Take a plane," said the first man.

The second man, however, looked me over as if I were a slab of meat. He wore a cook's smock and checkered pants stained with the wipes and spills of many meals.

"Well, you're no runaway," he said. "You're American, so you'd be running in the wrong direction."

"I'm just a boy on an adventure," I said.

"How old are you?"

"Sixteen," I lied.

"It just so happens I could use help in the galley. It's hard work."

"I don't mind."

The man pointed to a small container ship that might have been the oldest, rustiest thing afloat in Hong Kong harbor. The stern announced its name: MOBY KING.

"Passage in exchange for galley duty," said the man. "That's the deal."

"It's a deal," I said. "How many days does it take to sail to Seattle?"

"Thirteen," said the man.

"And do you know today's date?"

"Ninth of August. If you want the job, be here at oh six hundred hours. That's six a.m. sharp. Ask for Pap, the ship's cook. That's me."

I did some quick calculating. If I left Hong Kong on the tenth, I'd arrive in Seattle on August 22. I'd have a whole day to get to San Francisco. Seattle wasn't far from San Francisco, was it? Same coast, at least. I could do it. Just barely. Despite the detention center, despite the time-zone penalty, I could still make it around the world in forty days!

Jubilant, I ran back to Victoria Park.

"My luck has changed!" I shouted to the Buddha statue. "*Guinness Book of World Records*, here I come."

12:00.

I stashed my blue backpack and Reno tote bag behind a clump of bushes and took off to see the rest of Hong Kong.

Without money I couldn't do much. A cheap ferry chugged back and forth across the bay, and I rode it several times. I browsed through markets and window-shopped a lot. In a computer store that offered free Internet access, I e-mailed home.

Mom,

Camp is still fun, but I'm missing home. I'm learning how to play a game really well. You wanted me to get involved in activities, and that's what I'm doing. I've also met lots of interesting people. I look forward to August 23 and seeing you again.

Love, Adam

By dinnertime I had only enough money for a Happy Meal at McDonald's.

10:00 p.m.

I returned to Victoria Park, still on top of the world.

"Money's gone," I said aloud. "But who cares? Tomorrow I'll be on a ship headed home."

The park was well lit. Other backpackers were also sleeping rough on benches or on the grass.

As I walked toward the place where I had stowed my bags, a Chinese man in a suit and tie stopped me.

"Beware of teens with tubes," he said. "I spied them hiding in the bushes over there. They're staking out the blue backpack. If that's your gear, you're the person they're waiting for."

Stoppers! They must have tracked me to Hong Kong.

With a thank-you nod to the man, I stepped into a shadow. The entire GGG title was at stake. If I slept for twenty-four hours, I'd miss the boat.

Here was a tough decision to make. But, according to Radar, traveling was full of tough decisions.

Leaving my blue backpack and Reno tote bag behind, I turned and ran from the park.

I woke before the sun, chilly and covered with dew. My bed was a cement wall that ran along the harbor. Every bone in my skeleton ached—my clavicle, humerus, and radius, down to my tibia and fibula.

Two times during the night the Hong Kong police woke me up. Both times I walked to another section of the wall and returned to sleep. All night long, however, I worried more about stoppers with blowguns than about the police.

"Why can everyone in the GGG find me but my own team?" I wondered. "August 10. Day...question mark."

Along the harbor people did those slow tai chi exercises that Chinese people do in San Francisco. Nearby a sprinkler was spit-spit-spitting water onto the grass. After using the spray to clean my armpits, I hurried to the cargo pier.

Moby King was ready to sail. Containers now stood six high on the deck. Near the stern, a wide tower with revolving radar dishes on top rose above the stacks of boxes.

"Well, well, well, you made it after all," a voice called out. Pap was leaning over a rail. "What did you say your name was?"

A book we read in fifth grade, *Gulliver's Travels*, came to mind.

"Gulliver," I called out.

The cook smiled. "Well, Gulliver, come on board. There's plenty of KP work for you to do."

I climbed a flight of metal stairs and met Pap at the top. He wore the same stained chef's smock and pants. Slender and stooped, with a buzz haircut, he didn't fit my image of a ship's cook.

"Where's your gear, Gulliver?" he asked.

I shrugged.

"Ask no questions and I'll get no answers I don't want to hear," Pap replied.

He led me along a catwalk past several containers.

"What's in these things?" I asked.

"You name it, Gulliver. Sneakers, DVD players, sunglasses, Barbie dolls, squirt guns, car parts, T-shirts, Hula-Hoops, Christmas decorations, maybe even the pencils and erasers you'll use at school next fall."

I followed the cook though a door in the tower and down a flight of stairs. We entered a small dining room where three men were drinking coffee. Pap slapped a tall coffee urn on a counter.

"First rule of the ship's galley is to keep this big fella filled, Gulliver," he said. "Three crews run this ship on round-the-clock shifts. The crews run on coffee."

"Like teachers," I said.

I followed Pap into the narrow, dim kitchen. We passed an iron stove and had to duck under king-size kettles and pans hanging from hooks. Being a lunch lady's son, I'd been around jumbo cookware like this before.

"Stock pots, baking pan, spaghetti cooker, iron skillet, colander," I recited.

Pap gave a nod of approval.

Against the back wall stood a steel sink filled with crusty pots. Next to it was a round dishwasher.

"Here's your headquarters, Gulliver," the cook said. "The on button. The off button. If the red button blinks, dump dish soap in that box. Apron's hanging over there. You can begin by attacking those pots in the sink."

The ship lurched.

Pap picked up a large knife and began slicing potatoes. "Sweet to be at sea again," he said.

"Good-bye, Asia," I said through a yawn.

I hung the plastic apron over my neck. Attached to the sink was a long hose with a spray nozzle. I sprayed steaming water on a kettle and began scrubbing off burnt oatmeal with a wire brush.

Time Zones 18, 19, 20, 21, 22

That was my life for the next thirteen days. I rarely left the sink. I scrubbed pot after pot, pan after pan. I slid a zillion loads of dishes into the washer. As soon as I finished washing up for one meal, the crew began eating another.

At night I slept in a narrow berth in the crew's quarters. This was no luxury liner. It was a grimy, noisy,

diesel-spewing container ship, designed to carry stacks of boxes, not for the comfort of passengers. The sailors came from all over the world—Taiwan, Norway, the Philippines, Nigeria. Most of them knew only enough English to ask for more coffee.

Pap turned out to be an all right man. Born in South Dakota sixty years ago, he had been in the U.S. Navy most of his life.

"Nowadays I never travel far from the water," the cook said. "The steady earth feels funny under my feet."

Captain Abcdef ran the ship. He wore a frayed uniform, at one time white, now tinted pink. Short, squat, and sporting a stubby ponytail in his gray hair, the captain was the opposite of the cook. He was from Greece and hated the sea. According to Pap, bouts of seasickness were his curse.

"This'll be my final ocean crossing," I heard the captain tell Pap. "After Seattle I'm buying the driest plot of land in Greece I can find. It will be as far from the ocean as possible. Too many weird things happen at sea. I've seen the oddest storms, the wildest waves, and the strangest sea creatures while commanding the craziest crews."

During those pot-scrubbing days, I had plenty of time to think. I made plenty of mental lists.

Here's a list of things I wanted to learn when I got home:

1. How to speak French

2. How to speak Japanese
3. How to play a balalaika
4. How to play chess well
5. How to use chopsticks better
6. How to drive a motorboat

Here's a list of the things at home I missed most:

1. Mom's Toll House cookies
2. Curling up under my quilt
3. Saturday night videos with my mom
4. Eggs with mustard for breakfast
5. Listening to the radio
   (I'm sure I left it on in my bedroom)
6. An endless hot shower

Pap dropped a black kettle into the sink. "Need it scrubbed right away," he said, and my mind snapped back to work.

Whenever there was a break, I found fresh air by opening a door in the side of the ship. From there I looked out over the wrinkled ocean. In each new time zone (seven of them stretch across the Pacific), I flung a poker chip, like a tiny Frisbee, as far out to sea as possible.

On the eighth day out, I was standing at the open door when a black speck appeared on the horizon. The dot grew and grew until I realized what it was, a black helicopter aiming for *Moby King*'s deck. Where had I seen that chopper before? As it passed overhead, the TVP logo on the side became visible.

"Baron von Sheepsbottom, the Triton Voyage Project producer," I remembered. "What's he doing in the middle of the Pacific Ocean?"

Moments later, Captain Abcdef called through the galley's intercom, "Gulliver, come up to the bridge."

Pap whistled a long downward note. "Ask no questions and I'll get no answers I don't want to hear."

Time Zone 23, HDT (Hawaii Daylight Time)

For the first time during the sea voyage I climbed five flights of stairs to the ship's bridge. Captain Abcdef manned the helm. Baron von Sheepsbottom, dressed in black shorts, turtleneck, and boots, stood beside him. The walk from the helicopter across the windy deck had left his black beret cockeyed.

The baron smiled at me like a last-year's teacher. His square mustache spread into a trapezoid.

"There's the youthful traveler, my young adult adventurer, our junior explorer, at last," he said. "I've searched the world, seven continents and five oceans, for you."

"I keep getting found by the wrong people," I said.

Captain Abcdef looked my way. "Gulliver, why don't you step into my cabin with your uncle?"

"Uncle?" I peeped.

The baron placed a hand on my shoulder.

"Come along, young trekking nephew. We'll have a family chat."

My uncle? So that was Baron von Sheepsbottom's ruse. Why else would Captain Abcdef have allowed him on board? Either that or the baron had offered the right bribe. Curious, I followed the TVP producer into the captain's quarters behind the bridge.

The baron was all grins and friendly pats on the back. "So, Mr. Story, we've come near to the completion of our colossal cross-continental contest," he said. "You've been a fine player who's shown great potential, made excellent progress, and always displayed a positive attitude. A+ for effort. To tell you the truth, not one GGG producer thought you had the tiniest chance of winning this silly game. Now congratulations are in order. As of yesterday, you became the final player left in the Great Global Game."

This was surprising news, wonderful news if true. But I hardly trusted the baron.

"What happened to Meredith, the GVP player?" I asked.

"Your former companion was the twenty-second player eliminated," said the baron. "Typhoon Tutti-Frutti delayed her in Shanghai long enough for customs officials to find her."

"Meredith's home now?" I asked.

"She was a real trouper. The *GGG Daily News* gave a full account of a wild, all-day chase through Shanghai before authorities caught her and deported her home to LA."

"And what about your TVP player?"

"Number twenty-three to succumb," said the baron, shaking his head. "Chukudifu caught some cockamamie jungle fever in Columbia. Confounded doctors won't release him from their care for another fortnight."

"Does this mean I should call you Mr. von Sheepsbottom?" I asked.

The baron's toothbrush mustache twitched. "Uncle Gunter will do," he said.

"If this news is true, why didn't an MVP pilot fly here to tell me?" I asked.

"The fake Adam Story tracers I planted all over Asia have kept your MVP team far off track," Baron von Sheepsbottom said. "Your pilots searched for you everywhere except where you were."

"And the stoppers?" I said. "I suppose you hired them too."

The baron shrugged. "Ninety-nine of the most willful, wily, and wild bullies from ninety-nine different countries," he said. "All eager to chase twelve-year-olds around the globe."

"But I still can win this game. I just need to reach my school by noon on August 23."

The baron's smiled vanished. He tapped a bony finger against my chest. "And I swear by my ancestors' mustaches that that will never happen, Mr. Story," he snarled. "My great-great-great-great-great-great-great-grandfather was a great conqueror, a great hunter. The Sheepsbottom royal name won't be ended by a poor, fatherless loner, especially not one employed by Prince Oh."

"So why are you here?" I asked. "Are you going to offer me another bribe?"

"No more deals, Mr. Story," said the baron. "I flew to these forlorn coordinates where the wretched GGG referees wouldn't follow me. Game rules don't matter in the middle of the Pacific Ocean. I'm taking you to the –10 Detention Center in Hawaii."

The baron pulled a black GGG cell phone from his pocket. "Trackers, get ready," he said.

When we returned to the bridge, four trackers dressed in yellow turtlenecks and shorts stood by Captain Abcdef. My glance went from the trackers to the baron to the captain.

"Captain Abcdef, listen," I said. "My real name is Adam Story. I'm twelve years old and I'm the only remaining player in a huge international contest called the Great Global Game. I've traveled around the world from San Francisco, alone, and if I return home by August 23, I win four million dollars. Baron von Sheepsbottom is not my uncle. He's trying to stop me from winning the game so he can remain a baron."

The baron laughed, the trackers laughed, and the captain laughed. Even I thought my story sounded fishy.

Baron von Sheepsbottom grabbed my arm. "Come along, nephew," he said. "We'll be home in Hawaii in a few hours. It's only an adolescent phase he's going through, captain. Tall tales and all that."

I had to think fast. What proof did I have that my story was true? The black phone. Baron von Sheepsbottom still held the GGG satellite phone.

"Captain Abcdef, all I need to do is make one quick phone call," I said. "One call will convince you that everything I said is real."

"Fair enough, Gulliver," said the captain. "You can use *Moby King*'s ship-to-shore phone."

"No, I must use the cell phone that my phony uncle is packing."

Baron von Sheepsbottom released his hold on my arm. The alarm in his eyes told me that I'd nailed him.

"Enough nonsense," he said. "If you won't come with your uncle voluntarily, my assistants will carry you to the helicopter."

"That black phone is a special Great Global Game phone that works anywhere in the world, captain," I said. "By pressing M-V-P, I can connect to my team, the Magellan Voyage Project. Prince Oh, my producer, would be happy to talk with you."

"Very well, Uncle Gunter," Captain Abcdef said. "Let the boy use your phone."

Baron von Sheepsbottom made no reply. Instead, he started pushing his four trackers toward the exit.

"Move, move, you slackers!" he shouted. "We're wasting our time here."

His face crimson and his mustache twitching, the baron spun toward me. "You're a cheeky whipper-snapper, Mr. Story," he said. "By dumb luck you might make it to your final time zone. But by the time this rusty tub reaches Seattle, the docks will be crawling with trackers, hundreds of them. And don't forget my army of stoppers. They'll be hiding behind every tree and post waiting for you. By my ancestors' mustaches! By my ancestors' mustaches, Mr. Story, you won't see dear mommy again until after a long, deep sleep. Long after the Great Global Game is over."

A moment later, with a loud *Whump! Whump! Whump!,* the black helicopter rose from *Moby King*'s deck. Through the bridge window I watched it shrink to a tiny pill that dissolved on the horizon.

I turned to Captain Abcdef and shrugged. "Back to KP duty," I said.

The captain shook his head. "Weird things like this don't happen on dry land."

Time Zone 24, AKDT (Alaska Daylight Time)

Minutes later I sat with Captain Abcdef and Pap in *Moby King*'s dining room.

The cook chopped onions as he listened to my story.

"So let me get this all straight," Pap said. "You're all of twelve years old and have traveled all the way around the world, all by yourself." He wiped an onion tear from his eye. "And it's all part of a game all made up by all these ex-kings and queens."

"And it's almost all over," I said.

Captain Abcdef was suffering from seasickness. His pinkish shirt was unbuttoned, and his hand frequently went to his mouth to keep him from heaving.

"And that guy with the skinny legs wasn't your uncle?" the captain said. "Instead he's some endangered baron?"

I nodded. "The only evidence I have of circling the surface of the earth is the poker chips."

"Poker chips?" the captain and the cook said together.

I reached into my pocket and removed the final chip, a blue one. "I left a poker chip in every time zone I traveled through."

The cook wiped away another tear. "You know, Gulliver, I'm beginning to believe your big fish tale."

"What did the baron mean by trackers and stoppers waiting for you in Seattle?" asked the captain.

"Every team gets twenty-four trackers," I explained. "That means twenty-three times twenty-four...well, about five hundred and fifty trackers will be chasing me for the rest of the game. Baron von Sheepsbottom also hired a slew of teenagers to try and stop me."

Both the cook and captain stared at me watery-eyed. If I hadn't known about the onions and the seasickness, I'd have thought they were touched by my story.

"Well, Gulliver, maybe we have a solution to this hitch in your journey," Captain Abcdef said. "It just so happens that the *Moby King* needs to make a quick stop north of Seattle, prior to our scheduled arrival. We have some...*special* cargo to unload."

"Top-secret imports," Pap added. "That means we can drop you off without a soul knowing about it."

Something told me that this special cargo was more than used clothes. Ask no questions and I'll get no answers I don't want to hear, I thought to myself.

The plan sounded like a good one. Not only could I bypass trackers and stoppers, but also I could enter the United States without passport hassles. If I landed on the morning of August 22, if no referee spotted me, if I found the right transportation connections, I could be home before noon on August 23. Unbelievably, hope of winning the game was still alive.

Captain Abcdef left the dining room and then returned with an armful of clothing. "Put these on, Gulliver," he said. "Somehow, that black blowhard baron tracked you way out here in the ocean. Your clothes must contain a tiny transmitter. We'll toss your entire outfit over-board."

Good-bye to the T-shirt and jeans I'd worn for the past five weeks. Although it was a few sizes too big, the sailor's suit I put on—a blue pullover shirt and bell-bottom trousers—made me feel like part of the crew.

Two days later, the West Coast of America appeared through low morning fog. *Moby King* was trolling across the calm waters of Puget Sound. Having scrubbed my last breakfast pot, I stood with Pap on deck. In the bridge above us, Captain Abcdef pointed to starboard. Three black and white killer whales raced alongside the ship.

"Orca," Pap said. "Means good luck."

I nodded toward shore. "Home sweet home," I said. "That's where I can read the signs, speak the language, use familiar money, and say Fahrenheit instead of Celsius. Toilets work the way I expect, cars drive on the right side of the road, and people care about baseball."

Moby King anchored a few hundred yards off a secluded coastline. Instead of the Statue of Liberty or the Golden Gate Bridge to welcome me to America, a dirty white truck was parked on a narrow beach. Gliding out from the stony shore was a pontoon raft. In back, holding the tiller of an outboard motor, stood a brawny man with long carrot-colored hair tied in a ponytail. He wore bib overalls without a shirt, and tattoos covered every inch of his exposed skin up to his ears.

As I watched the pontoon boat approach, a sound on *Moby King*'s deck startled me. Horses' hooves! I turned to find four chocolate-colored horses standing there.

"Where'd they come from?" I asked Pap beside me.

"Gulliver, meet Clip-Clop, Flip-Flop, Hip-Hop, and Slip-Slop, four of the finest racehorses in China," he said. "They've been stabled in one of the containers for the past thirteen days. The crew has treated them well."

"They look in tip-top shape," I said. "So they're being smuggled into the United States?"

The cook nodded. "Ask no questions," he said. "I imagine they're worth a fortune to some horse breeder here."

Deckhands slipped slings under the horses' bellies and lowered them by crane onto the raft one by one.

"Your turn, Gulliver," Pap said. "Dog God will drive you to the Seattle train station."

"Dog God?" I said, staring down at the boat's skipper.

The man at the tiller had a mean appearance. His puffy lips wore the expression of a pouting kindergartner. His purple tattoos glistened in the morning sun.

"His bark is worse than his bite," the cook assured me.

Captain Abcdef walked up to me, holding out a wad of twenty-dollar bills. "This should get you home, Gulliver. Pay me back when you win your weird game."

"Thanks, captain," I said. "I'll visit you in Greece after I win. I'll just look for the driest spot."

Pap handed me some sugar cubes. "Travel well,

Gulliver," he called out. "We'll read about you, the world-famous traveler, in the newspaper."

I climbed down a rope ladder onto the pontoon boat. Clip-Clop, Flip-Flop, Hip-Hop, and Slip-Slop stood in the center of the flat deck.

I fed them sugar cubes and stroked their glossy coats.

"Welcome to America, fellas," I said.

Without a word Dog God started the motor and pushed the tiller, turning the raft toward shore. From this distance I could see his tattoos better. They were all of dogs. A bulldog crawled over one shoulder, and a poodle decorated the other. A dachshund sat under his armpit. His red ponytail in back swished across a German shepherd.

The morning was windless and the water flat. A crow cawed from a pine tree as if in greeting. The horses snorted a reply.

I checked my watch.

7:34.

"Tomorrow by noon, this will all be over," I said under my breath.

As we glided toward shore, Dog God remained silent. His stare stayed fixed on some distant point. No matter how hard I tried to avert my eyes, I remained focused on his tattoos. I spotted a beagle on his neck and a Great Dane on his chest.

The man's eyes met mine and narrowed. "What are you gawking at, Cracker Jack?" he snarled.

"Nothing," I said, and quickly turned toward Clip-Clop next to me.

Why did Dog God call me Cracker Jack? I wondered. My gaze fell upon the blue sailor's suit I wore. Right. I looked just like the boy on a box of Cracker Jack.

Part IV
North America Again

**"Home is where you know what to do
and how to do it."**

Time Zone 1, PDT (Pacific Daylight Time)

When I finally reached land, I felt like kissing the ground.
I felt like singing "America the Beautiful" or saying the
Pledge of Allegiance. But I
didn't. Not with Dog God
glaring at me. Instead, I
helped him lead the four
horses into the back of
the white truck.

Dog God and I sat in
the front seat with a pit
bulldog between us.
The dog's foamy chops
drooled ribbons of spit as he growled at me. He scowled
in the same manner as his master.

"Nice doggie," I said.

Dog God rubbed the bulldog's pointed ears. I noticed
a tattoo of a collie on Dog God's upper arm and a Saint
Bernard on his lower.

"Pup here likes people, Cracker Jack," he said. "It's kids he can't stand."

"Nice Pup. Nice doggie."

We began driving along a two-lane highway. After about a mile Dog God called out, "So, Cracker Jack, the captain mentioned you're part of the big game. I heard about the big game on the TV news."

"On the news?" I said astounded. "The Great Global Game was on the news?"

"Big scandal," Dog God said. "Some bigwigs were wagering on a big round-the-world race involving minors. Big bucks. They've rounded up some of the big cheese involved, an earl and a duchess. Big bust."

"What'd they say about the kids in the race?" I asked.

"TV news said they're all home safely now. That's why I was surprised when the captain radioed me about you, Cracker Jack."

I looked from Dog God to Pup, who was still growling and drooling, and back to Dog God. The basset hound tattoo on his throat rippled.

"So the Great Global Game could be canceled," I said. "No more teams. No more stoppers. No more rules."

"Big deal," Dog God said.

7:45.

The truck arrived at the Amtrak train station. Despite what the TV news had said, I checked for trackers before getting out.

"Good luck, Clip-Clop, Hip-Hop, Flip-Flop, and Slip-Slop," I called over my shoulder.

Pup growled, Dog God said nothing, and then once again I was alone.

Funny how Dog God's news hardly bothered me. The GGG prize money hadn't crossed my mind in weeks. I still had a goal. The challenge! The glory! Game or no game, I was within twenty-four hours of doing something no other twelve-year-old had ever done. One train ride and a BART ride would take me to the finish line. One day would complete my journey around the surface of the earth.

Inside the train station I bought a ticket to Oakland, California. The train departed at 10:00, so I had two hours to see Seattle.

The city was just waking up. People packed the streets, hurrying to work. At a Starbucks I bought a sticky roll and some orange juice. I took my breakfast and sat on a bench in a small, grassy park.

Quack! Quack! Quaaaaack!

A brown duck attracted my attention.

Quack! Quaaaaack! Quack! Quack! Quack!

The duck was waddling around a storm sewer at the edge of the park.

Quack! Quack! Quaaaaack!

Something was wrong. The duck was acting more like a worried mother than like a duck. She kept calling, flapping her wings, and circling the drainpipe.

I walked to the round sewer and peered through the iron grate that covered it. About eight feet down, six fuzzy ducklings were swimming in small O's and W's. A faint *cheep, cheep, cheep* reached my ears.

"So I see, Mom," I said to the mother duck. "Your babies fell through the grate."

Quack! Quack! Quaaaaack!

"I'll be right back."

I ran to the street. A policewoman in a blue and white uniform stood at the curb, writing a parking ticket for a yellow sport-utility vehicle.

"Over there!" I shouted. "Some baby ducklings are trapped in a sewer."

The policewoman slapped the ticket under the SUV's windshield wipers and said, "Let's go see."

We hurried back to the park. Having overheard me, a group of people followed. The mother duck was still quacking, and her chicks were still cheeping in the sewer.

The police officer spoke into a walkie-talkie Velcroed to her shoulder.

"Help can't get here for an hour," she told me. "This sewer drains into the bay. The little ducks could be swept away by then."

A cry of horror rose from the gathered people. A small man, who looked about eighty years old, knelt by the sewer. Although he appeared weak and frail, he reached down and pulled the iron grate right off.

The man looked up at me. "Come here, boy," he said. "How come we can't get those chicks out?"

I took a step backward.

"Come on. Come help," the man said. "Your size will come in handy."

I approached the sewer.

"Come get on your belly," said the man.

Lying on the grass, I drooped my head over the open drain. Phew! It smelled like the Dumpster outside my mom's kitchen. I reached down, but my fingers were still three feet above the ducklings.

The old man grabbed my ankles. "Come on. I'll lower you."

I slithered over the lip of the sewer to my waist. If he lost his hold, I'd take a header.

I inched forward some more. As my arms stretched out, something struck my ear. The last blue poker chip had fallen from my pocket. There it was, floating on the water near a duckling.

I cupped my hand and slid it under the chick.

"Got one!" I shouted, and the crowd above me erupted in cheers.

I cradled a second duck in my other hand. "Got another! Lift me up."

Soon I was sitting on the grass, releasing the wet, fuzzy balls. On big flat feet they zipped straight for their mother. The crowd, which had grown to a few hundred, rooted and clapped their hands.

"Let's keep them coming," the old man called to me.

It took two more trips down the sewer to rescue all the ducklings. At last, I stood and brushed off my jeans.

Quack! Quaaaaack! Quack! Quack!

The mother duck led her brood into the bushes.

A TV news van had arrived to film the scene. Now the cameraman pointed his camera at me, and a woman held out a microphone.

"What's your name? How old are you? Where are you from? What school do you go to?" she asked.

What was I doing? I couldn't be seen on TV! If the GGG was banned and someone recognized me, I'd be in trouble as a player. If the game was still running, every tracker in the world would zero in on this spot. And most important, I had a train to catch.

"Do you have the time?" I asked the policewoman, who was holding back the crowd.

"Two until ten," she said.

I took off. Ducking low, I plowed through the crowd and sprinted all the way to the train station. I arrived panting hard. A man in a blue uniform stood beside the departure door marked COAST STARLIGHT.

"Is that the train to Oakland?" I asked, still catching my breath.

"Twas," the man answered. "Train pulled out five minutes ago. There'll be another one tomorrow."

Tomorrow? Tomorrow would be too late. I couldn't wait until tomorrow.

I called the Greyhound bus station.

"Bus to San Francisco leaves at 4:30 p.m.," a computer voice told me. "It arrives at 12:15 p.m. the next day."

Unbelievable. I had traveled twenty-six thousand miles around the world, and the last eight hundred had me stumped.

Only one option was left, risky in both safety and time. Since Interstate 5 passed by Seattle and continued south through Oregon and California, I could hitchhike. If I was lucky with rides, if trackers didn't find me, if the police left me alone—if, if, if—maybe I could make it to the picnic table on time.

Outside the station I found a sheet of cardboard. I entered a Starbucks to borrow a pen. While I was writing SF in fat black letters, a woman with blond hair dangling over her laptop computer looked my way.

"You hitching to San Francisco?" she asked.

"I'm gonna try," I said.

"Can't you take a bus or a train?" said the woman.

"Too hard to explain. I just have to be home by Friday noon."

"Listen, do you need to borrow money?"

"Thanks, but money wouldn't help me now."

"But the police won't let you stand on the highway ramps near the city center."

"I gotta risk it."

"Listen," the woman said, closing her computer, "let me take you to a safe place on the freeway to stand."

This was the first break I had had since I got to America. The woman's name was Elle, and she was studying to be a teacher at the University of Washington. We drove in her old Honda to a freeway on-ramp south of the city.

"Listen, will you be all right?" she asked as I got out.

I nodded and watched the Honda drive away.

Phoot! Phoot! Two cars flew by.

I held up my "SF" sign.

Phoot! Phoot! Phoot! Another car, a pickup truck, and a delivery van.

I stuck the sign straight out. I waved it. I raised it over my head. I flapped it like a flag. How could anyone resist me?

Phoot! Phoot! Phoot! Phoot!

"This won't be easy," I said aloud.

2:00 by my watch. Twenty-two hours left.

Phoot! Phoot!

Traffic passed along with the hours.

3:00. 4:00.

I counted cars. I played the state license plate game that I played with Mom on long car trips.

5:00. 6:00.

Still I waited. Still I waved my sign. But no car stopped. Happy parents with happy children appeared in car windows, probably headed home to happy houses. No one cared about me.

7:00.

I was hungry. I was bored. Could things get any worse? Lots. Around 7:30, I felt the first bout of something Radar had warned me about.

"You can call it Delhi Belly, Montezuma's Revenge, Pharaoh's Curse, Turkish Two-Step, Traveler's Trots," he'd said. "If you travel a lot, sooner or later you're going to get it. Good old diarrhea."

I ran into the bushes.

8:00. 9:00.

The sun sank along with all hope of reaching home in time. A streetlight turned on, and I sat on the guardrail in the pool of light.

"Not enough time," I told myself. "All this for nothing."

I had toured the world. I had faced dangers, dreary nights, delays, and deceptions. Now the forty-day deadline would pass a few hours too soon.

I had lost the challenge.

That's when I did something I hadn't done in years. My vision blurred with tears. My face dropped into my hands, and I bawled like a two-year-old.

A car honked. Elle's Honda had pulled up beside me.

"I was worried about you," Elle called out the window.

"Listen, come crash at my apartment tonight? I'll bring you back here in the morning."

I rubbed away tears with the back of my hand. "Tomorrow will be too late."

"What's the rush?" Elle asked. "I thought you didn't need to be home until Friday."

"That's right."

"But tomorrow's Thursday."

I leaped to my feet. "Thursday? Tomorrow's not August twenty-third?"

"The twenty-second," said Elle.

My mind was racing. How was this possible? How did I miss a day?

"The International Dateline!" I shouted. "*Moby King* crossed the International Dateline! I gained twenty-four hours!"

I started dancing around the circle of streetlight.

"No one mentioned the day all day!" I called out. "This is Day 38! Not 39!"

Elle sat in her car looking confused.

"I'm back in the game!" I shouted. "I have a chance! I can win! I have a whole new day!"

From the moment I got into Elle's car, I began babbling about the Great Global Game. Elle had read about it in the Seattle newspaper. She was impressed that I was still a contestant.

"Listen, let's get some dinner," she said. "I've never eaten with a celebrity before."

Elle drove to a café that had four big semi trucks parked outside. We sat in a booth with cracked red vinyl seats. The server brought us hamburgers and French fries.

"I thought I'd lost the game," I said while eating. "That's why I went nuts when you told me tomorrow is Thursday."

Elle shook her head. "All this for some rich aristocrats' amusement," she said. "Any one of you kids could have gotten injured or terribly ill or captured by terrorists. I'm glad they're locking up every member of that League of Royalty without Domains. You're twelve, right? Weren't you scared being out there alone?"

"Not really," I said.

"Weren't you lonely?"

"Hardly ever." And I started to name all the traveling companions I'd had in the past six weeks.

Elle looked around the café. "Listen, I think I know a safe and fast way for you to get to San Francisco. Come with me."

We walked to a booth in the back of the café. A large white-haired woman sat there eating apple pie. She wore wraparound sunglasses even though it was nighttime. Her denim shirt had an American flag on the back.

"Martha, are you driving south tonight?" Elle asked her. "Adam needs a ride to San Francisco."

"Sure, he don't look too harmful," the woman said. She stuck out a hand that I shook. "Truckers call me Mom, honey. As soon as I finish my pie we'll be on our way."

I thanked Elle and sat in the vinyl seat across from Mom. Three empty pie plates on the table told how many pieces she'd already polished off.

"Let's hit the road," she finally said.

After a quick trip to the toilet, I followed Mom to the parking lot. Her truck was an eighteen-wheeler painted red, white, and blue. American flags adorned the front grille and mud flaps. A small flag drooped from the antennae. The license plates read: GIRL RIG.

Mom opened the cabin door. "Other side, honey," she said.

I raced around the back of the truck. As I passed the canvas American flag that covered the rear, a ferocious growl nearly knocked me off my feet.

"Not too close," Mom warned me.

I scrambled into the cabin. "What's back there?"

"Movie animals. I'm hauling a mountain lion, a badger, a bear cub, and an old barn owl. I deliver animals to film sets all across America. They must be making a wilderness movie near San Francisco."

The cabin seats were red, white, and blue leather. The

dashboard was striped red and white, and white stars spangled the blue roof. Another American flag hung behind us.

"Thanks for the lift," I said. "This is great."

Mom started the diesel engine. "No problem, honey. I ain't much of a talker, though."

Soon we were trucking down Interstate 5. Now my school, the finish line, was just one long ribbon of asphalt away, I-5 to I-505 to I-80.

Mom drove without speaking. Maybe from excitement, maybe from being alone all day, I couldn't keep my mouth shut. I began reading signs aloud.

"San Francisco 780 miles.

"Maximum speed 70.

"Rest area two miles.

"Olympia next five exits."

Mom pushed a CD into the truck's player. The cabin filled with country music. A guy sang about America and missing his girlfriend.

"Olympia's the capital of Washington," I said. "I can name every state capital. Salem, Oregon. Sacramento, California. Carson City, Nevada. Phoenix, Arizona. Look, that sign says Mount Rainier. Wanna hear a list of all the ten-thousand-foot peaks in the Cascades? Mount Rainier, Mount Shasta, Mount Adams, Mount Hood..."

"Honey, why don't you go on back and get some sleep?" said Mom. "It's almost midnight."

"In back with the mountain lion?"

"No, pull aside Old Glory behind you."

I lifted a corner of the flag and discovered a small sleeping space with a narrow bed.

"Cool," I said. "Do you want to hear a list of all the strange beds I've slept in during the past six weeks? A bus seat, a train sleeper, a king-size bed at The Plaza, another one on the QM2..."

Mom cranked up the music and I got the message. I climbed into the cubby and stretched out.

"Night, Mom."

"Night, honey."

I lay there listening to the music and the *shhhhhhh* of the highway beneath me.

"Things work out," I reminded myself.

Day 39.

Sunlight streamed through the American flag wall of my little room. Morning had come, but something was wrong. The truck was stopped. In back, the mountain lion roared, the bear growled, and the owl hooted.

I flipped the flag aside and saw no driver. The truck was parked in a grass field surrounded by oak trees.

"Mom, where are you?" I shouted.

I leaped from the truck cabin. Across the field a large RV camper was parked. Twice as long and wide as Mom's semi, it was the largest RV I'd ever seen. Outside the camper, a beach umbrella shaded a patio table and chairs. The black helicopter standing behind it explained a lot.

"Baron von Sheepsbottom has been up to something," I concluded.

Sprawled on the grass under the trees were stoppers, twenty of them. The teenagers now wore shiny red running shorts, shirts, and shoes. Again each one had a large white number on the back. Number 93 was chomping on a hard-boiled egg. Number 52 whittled on his blowgun with a pocketknife, while Numbers 72 and 73 played cards. The instant I stepped forward, Numbers 27 and 15 leaped to their feet.

"Let him pass, boys," a voice commanded from the camper.

A screen door opened and out stepped Baron von Sheepsbottom. He wore shiny black pajamas along with his black beret.

"Greetings once again, Mr. Story, our last vagabond, our final wanderer, our lone remaining rover," he said. His square mustache wavered from side to side. "Welcome to my, shall we say, *private* TVP Detention Center."

"What have you done, baron?" I demanded.

The baron chugged some coffee from the mug he held.

"You were so, so close, Mr. Story," he said. "So close to home and victory, but, alas, so far away. Late last night my teenaged recruits hijacked your truck. They'll detain you only until it's impossible for you to reach home by noon tomorrow."

"Where's the driver? Where's Mom?"

The baron held open the RV door. "Right this way."

I stepped inside the camper. When my eyes adjusted

to the dimness, they took in a sight that made me want to puke. Along the walls hung mounted heads of animals, ones that I had admired on the Net—a gazelle, an impala, a zebra, a jaguar, a timber wolf, a grizzly bear... I couldn't bear to see what else.

"Notice the rare Siberian tiger rug on the floor," Baron von Sheepsbottom said, wiping his feet on the animal's neck. "Above us, wings from the world's most endangered birds cover the ceiling. Look, there are the feathers of a California condor I shot yesterday."

Feeling the stares of all those marble eyes, I followed the baron to the middle of the camper.

"Check out the sofa. Upholstered with one hundred percent hippopotamus leather," he went on. "And those pillows? Yes, that's natural panda fur. The legs of the table are authentic elephant legs, the armchair has genuine orangutan arms, and the footstool, yes, that's a real gorilla foot. Bagged the beasts myself. And see the Jacuzzi in the rear? Those handles are actual chimpanzee hands. Very handy."

Beside the tub, Baron von Sheepsbottom pointed out Mom asleep on a bed lined with crocodile hide.

"Miss America will snooze for a day," he explained. "I believe you're acquainted with the sleeping juice my stoppers apply to the tips of their blowgun darts. I tapped the sap from rare trees in Lapland. Oh, and listen to this."

The baron stepped up to the driver seat and pressed the center of the steering wheel. Out came the hideous scream of a hyena.

"My RV's horn was carved from an actual rhinoceros horn," he said.

I was about to bolt from the Camper of Horror when I spied a copy of *GGG Daily News* #39 on the table. The headline read:

MVP PLAYER VANISHES!
Great Drama as Game Enters Final Day

"I thought the law shut down the Great Gross Game," I said.

Baron von Sheepsbottom grinned. "Oh, LORD members fed the press some gossip to keep things interesting," he said. "But rest assured, Mr. Story, no law can touch us royals. We are above the law, all law, any international laws, and laws of any country. We never need passports, permits, permission to go anywhere or do anything on earth."

The TVP producer clapped his hands twice, and two stoppers sprang into the camper.

"Bring our guest his breakfast," he ordered. "I believe eggs with mustard is his preference. If Mr. Story can't be at home, he can at least enjoy some of its pleasures."

I ate in the shade of Mom's truck. In the distance, traffic hummed on Interstate 5. The hills and cliffs around me were familiar. My mother and I had camped the summer before in this part of Northern California, near Lake Shasta.

"Too many stoppers around for me to make a run for the highway," I told myself. "Escaping from here will be a challenge."

My belly cramped. Diarrhea remained a problem. When I headed into the bushes, four stoppers, Numbers 8, 35, 90, and 22, grabbed their blowguns and followed me.

As I said, I knew this area well. I could name every tree, wildflower, and shrub. On my trips into the bushes near the RV site, there was one plant with three-fingered jagged leaves that I kept having to detour around. Poison oak. It grew everywhere, in big clumps and bushes. To my surprise, the bare-legged, bare-armed stoppers walked right through it.

Suddenly an escape plan unfolded.

"Right now diarrhea and poison oak might be my best friends," I said. "Leaves of three, let them be—but not me."

I spent the rest of the morning sitting in Mom's truck, listening to CDs. I made frequent trips to the bushes. Each time four stoppers accompanied me. Each time I purposely went past as much poison oak as possible. I detoured around the plants, but the teenagers continued to brush against them.

Late that afternoon Baron von Sheepsbottom exited his RV with a shotgun crooked under his armpit.

"I heard that a few bald eagles remain in these parts, Mr. Story," he called out. "America's national bird. Wouldn't that make a fine trophy for my camper?"

I sat up in Mom's driver's seat. "Isn't shooting an eagle illegal?"

"Not for the regal," the baron replied. "May I remind

you, Mr. Story, no laws can touch us privileged people with noble names. We hunt where we want, when we want, and what we want."

As the producer strode from the campsite, I told myself, "Another urgent reason to escape and win the Great Groovy Game. Without a royal title, the ex-baron would be put behind bars for poaching. Wildlife would be saved. My diarrhea, you might say, is for the birds."

An hour later, to my relief, the baron returned empty-handed. Not long afterward, the stoppers began to scratch. My plan was working. All twenty teenagers were running fingernails over bare arms and legs as they sat on the grass.

"You out there, be still!" Baron von Sheepsbottom called from the RV. "I'm paying you to watch the player, not to fidget."

The camper's rear window framed the baron, soaking in the Jacuzzi. Mom remained asleep on the bed.

"The stoppers don't even know what hit them," I said. "As I figured, since they're not from around here, their bodies haven't developed any resistance to the poison oak sap."

I started into the brush again. Four stoppers followed.

"Time for more of Adam Story's revenge," I sang out.

That night the stoppers made a campfire. From experience, I knew that this was good for me and bad for them. Heat makes poison oak itching worse. The stoppers stood around the fire, scratching all over. Their blowguns served as backscratchers.

"Ayyyyy!" they cried. "Eeeee! I-I-I-I-I! Ohhhhh! Ewwwww!"

By 10:00, every teenager was twisting, writhing, and rolling on the ground. Bumpy rashes already covered their bodies. Many had swollen faces.

"Ayyyyy! Eeeeee! I-I-I-I-I! Ohhhhh! Ewwwww!"

From the truck cabin I watched the scene. The stoppers hopped around the fire in Rumpelstiltskin fashion. Backlit, they appeared in silhouette, shadow puppets with flailing arms and legs.

"Ayyyyy! Eeeeee! I-I-I-I-I! Ohhhhh! Ewwwww!"

"Time to leave," I said.

I opened the truck door and dropped to the ground. A leap out of the firelight would make me invisible. Done. Through inky blackness I ran, stumbling over rocks and bumping into trees. Behind me, the stoppers continued to wail.

"Ayyyyy! Eeeeee! I-I-I-I-I! Ohhhhh! Ewwwww!"

Twenty minutes of running still brought no sign of Interstate 5. I stopped and listened. Nothing. I couldn't recall a quieter moment. The North Star in the right-hand sky, however, told me that my direction was correct. Looking back, I thought of Gunter the Hunter.

"What a prize I'd be for his RV," I said, taking off again.

I ran; I tripped; I ran some more. Finally, from a cliff, I spotted white headlight beams in the distance. I-5! More tripping and tumbling followed as I scrambled toward the moving bright lines. Once I got to the freeway, I climbed over the wire fence and up a dirt embankment until I was standing on the gravel shoulder. A pair of headlights stared at me, and I stuck out my thumb.

Phhhhhooooom!

The car blew past with a blast of wind.

Again and again, headlights flooded over me. Suddenly a new beam, a single white shaft, shot down from the sky. It struck the freeway a hundred yards to the north and formed a bright circle on the pavement. The white disc slid along the southbound lane, drawing closer and closer to where I stood.

Whump! Whump! Whump!

"Hello, Mr. von Sheepsbutt," I said.

Although I heard the helicopter, it remained invisible against the black sky. Just as the searchlight reached me, I leaped off the shoulder and slid down the embankment. I crawled into a steel culvert the size of a Hula-Hoop.

Whump! Whump! Whump!

The chopper was overhead. The white beam paused at the culvert's entrance. I crawled farther into the tube. Back and forth the light wobbled.

"Mr. Story, come out, come out, wherever you are!" the baron called through a loudspeaker. His voice echoed through the metal pipe. "I swear by my ancestors' mustaches, I'll not harm you. Let's be pals. I'm offering you four million dollars to quit the game right now. OK, five million! Olly-olly oxen free, Mr. Story! Who cares about a silly little game anyway? Six million, and that's my final offer."

At last the light slid away, but I dared not leave my hiding place. Balled up, with my bleeding knees to my chin, I would spend the night in the culvert.

From deep within the pipe something rustled, a wild creature perhaps also seeking shelter. At least the place was dry.

"Tomorrow, my own bed," I told myself.

Day 40. August 23. 6:00 a.m.

Cramped and sore, I stood on Interstate 5, thrusting my thumb toward each passing car. I tilted my head back. No black helicopter. The sky was solid blue, Royal Blue.

Phooooom! Phooooom!

Twenty yards down the road, a green sign read: SAN FRANCISCO 221 MILES.

On the sign sat a single crow.

"This is the endgame, bird," I said. "The last inning, the final period, the two-minute warning. If I don't get a ride within the next two hours, the game's all over, finished, kaput."

As I spoke, a red pickup pulled off the pavement. Bales of hay filled the back.

"Get in, young fella," said the driver, who wore a battered straw hat and had tufts of straw-colored hair in his ears.

The driver was a cattle rancher named Bob. Bob drove slowly, more slowly than I could spit. The speedometer rarely went over 40 miles per hour.

Bob talked as slowly as he drove. "So, ah, where are you, ah, headed, young fella?" he asked.

"San Francisco. I need to be there in a hurry."

"What's, ah, your rush?" Bob asked. "You young fellas, ah, are all in a hurry these days. I suspect the, ah, chopper back there was a traffic patrol, ah, checking for speeders."

I slumped in my seat. "How far are you going?" I asked.

"Ah, Red Bluff. About twenty miles, ah, down the road."

7:10 by my watch. The numbers on the truck's odometer circled at a crawl. I pressed my right foot against the floorboard, as if that would make the truck go faster.

Eighteen miles later, Bob put on his blinkers and rolled up the Red Bluff exit. I was out of the truck before it stopped.

8:16.

"Thanks," I shouted.

"Ah, slow down, young fella," Bob said. "We have, ah, all the time in the world, ah, to get to where, ah, we're, ah, going."

I raced back to the freeway, pumping my thumb up and down.

The next car, a yellow convertible, pulled over.

"I gotta get to San Francisco fast," I called to the driver.

"I'm going to San Francisco fast, amigo," he replied.

This driver's name was Oro, and he was about twenty. Oro pressed a button, and the canvas top of the car went back.

"Could you leave the top up?" I asked.

"No offense," Oro said, "but you smell really bad."

I sniffed my armpits and had to agree. Scooching far down in my seat, I scanned the sky. Still no black helicopter.

"Fasten your seatbelt, amigo," Oro said. "Here we go."

With a blast of gravel, the convertible tore off the shoulder. It flew down I-5. This was more like it. Eighty miles per hour all the way.

Racecar, I thought. My favorite palindrome.

I counted the mile markers as they whizzed by.

"Forty-seven...forty-eight...forty-nine."

The wind in the roofless car ruined any chance of a conversation.

"Sixty-one...sixty-two."

9:00, according to the dashboard clock.

"One hundred and three...one hundred and four."

10:06.

We turned off I-5 onto I-505.

A green sign read: SAN FRANCISCO 88 MILES.

Never had miles seemed so long and minutes so short.

10:19.

Oro turned up an exit ramp.

"What did you do that for?" I shouted.

"Relax, amigo. Need to make a quick phone call."

We pulled into a McDonald's. Oro got out to use the phone. This was torture. Unable to sit still, I got out too and paced around the car. "Come on, come on, come on!"

Finally Oro returned. "Fasten your seatbelt," he said, and the race against time continued.

10:37.

Interstate 505 melted into Interstate 80, the same highway on which I started this journey forty days before. The two lanes with a row of white bumpy things between them became four lanes, and Oro really took off.

A green sign read: SAN FRANCISCO 46 MILES.

I dared look at the clock.

11:02.

Less than an hour remained. At school I'd watch the clock and beg for noon, lunchtime, to come. Now my one wish was for time to stand still.

"If I'm not home by twelve, you wouldn't believe what I'll miss," I called to Oro.

The driver smiled and squeezed down the gas pedal.

11:15.

Home territory now. We flew past Exit 16, which went to the mall. We sailed by Exit 17, which led to my apartment. Exit 18 headed nowhere that I knew, but Oro put on his blinkers and veered up the off-ramp.

"This isn't it," I shouted. "I gotta go one more exit."

The car crunched to a stop at the side of the road.

"This *is* it, amigo," Oro said. "BART station is over there."

11:21.

I leaped from the car and sprinted toward the station. With my last two dollars I bought a ticket. I charged up the escalator two steps at a time.

"Come, BART, come," I pleaded, pacing the platform. "Come on, come on, come on."

I waited and waited. My heart did a loud thumping job beneath my sailor's shirt.

11:26.

The long silver train rounded a bend in the track. Why was it moving so slowly? It crawled to a halt before me and I jumped on. The graffiti on the ceiling was familiar. This was the same BART car I'd been on forty days before.

The door closed, but the train remained put.

"Attention, BART passengers," an intercom voice called out. "Due to a dog on the track ahead, we'll be delayed momentarily at this station."

"No, no, no!" I groaned.

My eyes never left my watch. Having set it to the playground bell at the game's start, I knew it was accurate.

11:30.

11:31.

11:32.

Finally, finally, the BART train slunk forward. At the next station I bolted off and leaped down the escalator four steps at a time.

Outside the station entrance, a small girl wearing a large mushroom bike helmet had just ridden up on a one-gear bicycle.

"I need your bike!" I yelled. "It's an emergency! Please! Please!" Not waiting for an answer, I ripped the handlebars from the girl's grip.

"Well...I guess," she said.

I flew out of there.

11:47.

My knees pumped up and down like car pistons. The bike was so small they nearly hit my arm.

"Go, go, go, go!" I shouted.

I pedaled down Minor Street. I pedaled down Major

Street. The bike took a corner in a skid. Down another street, a turn, down another street, and past the Wells Fargo Bank.

11:53.

The school appeared in the distance. A school bus was parked in front, bringing kids back from camp.

"Go, go, go, go!"

11:56.

I tore into the parking lot. My mom's VW was parked near the bus. Mom was there to pick me up, but she didn't see me zoom in behind her.

11:57.

"Go, go, go, go!" I rounded the side of the school and sped onto the playground.

11:58.

The bell! The bell! The recess bell would ring at twelve o'clock.

11:59.

I reached the After-School Club building and leaped off the bike. "Don't ring! Don't ring! Don't ring!"

Was that man in the bushes wearing a striped kaffiyeh? I didn't stop to find out. I sprinted toward the picnic table, the finish line.

"Don't ring! Don't ring!"

In one swift motion, I stepped on the table bench and sprang onto the wooden tabletop. Regaining my balance, I stood up straight. I raised my arms above me in a V.

"Home!" I shouted.

Riiiiiiiiiiiiiiiiiiiiiiiiiiiiiiiiiiing!

Game over! Finished! Ta-daaa! That was it!

No one cheered; no one clapped. No one took my picture or even came to congratulate me. I checked the bushes, but no man stood there.

"Well done, Adam," I said to myself, and climbed down from the table.

I strolled over to the school bus in the parking lot. Mingling with the crowd, I pretended to be a returning camper.

Mom beeped her car horn. "Yoo-hoo, Adam!" she yodeled out the window. "Hurry up. I'm late for work."

She never mentioned my lost luggage. She never mentioned my sailor's suit, the scrapes on my arms, or my BO. Her mind was on cleaning houses.

First thing back in my apartment, I went to my bedroom and turned off the radio. It had been playing at low volume for forty days.

Afterwards, I was restless. I switched on the TV, but I couldn't watch it. I wanted to keep moving. I needed to share my story with someone, but no one was around who would listen. Who would have believed me anyway? I picked up the newspaper but found no mention of the Great Global Game scandal. I began to doubt that I'd even taken the trip.

The following week, I started at the middle school. Even though my mother worked in the cafeteria, no one paid much attention to me. The school was huge, and only two former classmates were in my homeroom.

Days were uneventful; nothing happened. Instead of doing homework during my study halls, I wrote down every detail of my forty-day journey on a school computer.

One afternoon the mail carrier delivered a picture postcard to our apartment. The card, from Meredith Emerson, showed a cheesy picture of a "jackalope," a giant make-believe rabbit with antlers. It read:

Adam,

I found your address on the Internet. My parents are building a highway in Nevada, so we moved to a town called Warm Springs. There are no springs here, and it's not warm. It's hot! I lost the GGG in China. Did you make it? E-mail me.

Travel well,

Madam

Meredith's e-mail address appeared at the bottom of the card. My e-mail reply to her said:

Meredith,

I made it around the world in thirty-nine days, twenty-three hours, fifty-nine minutes, and fifty-eight seconds. But who cares?

Adam

Later that month, when I arrived home from school, a red, white, and blue Federal Express mail pouch lay on our doormat. It was addressed to me. No return address.

I ripped open the cardboard envelope and dumped the contents on our dining room table. Fifteen poker chips dropped out.

"Who sent poker chips?" Mom asked.

"Dunno. There's no letter."

I turned the packet upside down and shook it. Out fell a small slip of paper. A California lottery ticket.

The date on the ticket told me that the ticket had been bought this week. That meant the winning numbers were announced in today's newspaper.

I opened the paper to the lottery section. I compared the numbers drawn in the Super Lotto Plus with the numbers on my ticket.

First number, the same. Second number, same. Third, fourth, and fifth numbers, all matched. I double-checked the newspaper and double-checked my ticket.

"Ka-ching! Ka-ching! Ka-ching!" I shouted.

I had just won four million dollars.